My grandmother had my mum a bit early, then decided to get married later on. Babies upset everything – baths, plates of food and relationships. But sometimes (not always) the love they bring changes everything too – for the better.

Lisa Drakeford tells a warm, funny, wise story that will keep you guessing about what effect one little bundle has on friendship – and everything!

[signature]

BARRY CUNNINGHAM
Publisher
Chicken House

the baby

lisa drakeford

Chicken House

2 Palmer Street, Frome, Somerset BA11 1DS

www.doublecluck.com

Text © Lisa Drakeford 2015
First published in Great Britain in 2015
Chicken House
2 Palmer Street
Frome, Somerset BA11 1DS
United Kingdom
www.doublecluck.com

Lisa Drakeford has asserted her right under the Copyright, Designs and Patents
Act 1988 to be identified as the author of this work.

Cover and interior design and illustration by Helen Crawford-White
Typeset by Dorchester Typesetting Group Ltd
Printed and bound in Great Britain by CPI Group (UK) Ltd, Croydon CR0 4YY

The paper used in this Chicken House book is made from wood grown in
sustainable forests.

1 3 5 7 9 10 8 6 4 2

British Library Cataloguing in Publication data available.

ISBN 978-1-910002-23-0
eISBN 978-1-910002-24-7

For Dan Tunstall. So sad that you'll never read this.

And for a real-life Olivia – nothing like my fictional one.
She's had a rubbish year and I've been so proud and
impressed at the way she's handled it.
I promised her mum I'd keep an eye out for her.
This book is to make you smile, Olivia H.

olivia february

'Don't disturb Mrs Greasly next door. You know how cross she gets about noise late at night.' Her mum tugs with anxious fingers at her handbag.

'I know.' Olivia nods.

'And don't excite Sandy.'

'She'll be with Alice.'

Her dad jingles his car keys.

'Use the carpet spray under the sink if you spill anything.' Her mum loiters on the doorstep. Olivia's dying to close the door.

'I will.'

'Oh, and remember Alice. Check on her, won't you? You know how scared she gets with strangers.'

Olivia stares at the doormat, tracing patterns with her toe. *Just go, will you?*

'And make sure she gets something to eat.' Her mum's eyes narrow. 'You won't let anything horrible happen to her, will you?'

Olivia wants to scream. It fizzes in her stomach. 'Course not.'

She throws a look at her dad, begging him to drag her mum away to the restaurant. Why is it always, *always* like this? Why, even at her seventeenth birthday party, are they still worrying about her sister? It makes her so mad. Why is it *still* about Alice?

But she takes a breath and sticks a smile on her face.

'She'll be fine. I'll keep an eye on her. She's not been sick all day now.' It's typical of her sister to be recovering from a bug at the worst possible moment.

She sees her mum look nervously over at her dad who shrugs and points the key at the car. Olivia sighs and half closes the door. *Please go. Please just go.*

At last!

She closes her eyes with relief when her mum snaps shut her handbag and makes steps towards the car.

But it's difficult to ignore the anxious look from her mum up towards Alice's bedroom window.

The door crunches closed and she takes the stairs up to her room two at a time. It's actually happened; after moaning and grumbling for the best part of two weeks now, her parents have finally left her to it.

At the top of the stairs she lets her shoulders sag, feels a lift in her chest, starts to smile. *Let's get this party started!*

'God, I'm so fat.' Nicola grimaces in the mirror, spreads her fingers across her belly and bends over towards the iPod for music.

She's dressed in leggings and a long 'I ♥ NY' vest top. There's a half-finished bottle of cider on the floor beside her.

'Don't be stupid. You look lovely.'

Nicola groans and jabs her stomach. 'There's nothing lovely about this.'

Olivia attends to her mascara, her mouth open with focus. 'Shut up, Nic – it's just Christmas weight. We've all got it. It takes three days to gain and three months to lose.'

Nicola shakes her head, unconvinced. 'So where's yours?'

Olivia sifts through her make-up bag. There's a rattle of tubes and applicators between her fingers. 'Well disguised, underneath this.' She tugs at her top, pulling it over her bum.

Nicola shrugs and averts her eyes. Olivia shakes her head. Her friend's always been the same. She's the original yo-yo dieter. Ever since Olivia's known her, from the age of seven, she's been unhappy with how she looks. She's seen Nic gain and lose weight at the drop of a hat and Nic's never satisfied with the result. And tonight, just like every other night, Olivia thinks Nic looks lovely. She's curvy in the right places, unlike Olivia who's more straight up and down. Nicola's hair is glossy and long, winding around her shoulders. Her mum describes it as her 'crowning glory.' She has a pretty face with a heart-shaped mouth, which is enough to have boys falling over themselves for her attention. Only she has no idea. So frustrating. She has no confidence in her looks.

There's nothing Olivia can say; she's said it all before. But even so, she slips her hands on Nicola's shoulders, breathes in her musky smell and smiles at the image in the mirror. 'Nic – you look great. Gorgeous.' She catches Nic's brown eyes. 'You're my best friend, my oldest friend, and I wouldn't have you any other way. And when you're working for Versace you've got to remember me.' Nicola has massive aims to work for a top designer when she's older and Olivia's sure that she can do it. Her taste in fashion is brilliant.

Nicola frowns, lowering her eyes. Embarrassed. Her voice catches so it comes out as a husk. 'You know I'll always remember you. And you look amazing too. You do all the time. I love that top.'

Olivia pulls at it. 'Do you think?' Pouts. 'I'm not so sure. Jonty hates it. Says it's too low cut.'

Nicola sighs. 'Don't listen to him. If it was up to him he'd have you in a nun's outfit.' She turns towards Olivia and checks her friend's face.

Olivia feels like she's being weighed up by an elite fashion stylist. It's nice. She respects Nicola's opinion. She waits while Nicola wipes at Olivia's eyelid with a brush. 'You spend too long worrying about what he's going to say.'

Olivia feels a disappointed lump develop in her throat. Turns towards the cider bottle, suddenly wanting more. 'Habit, I guess,' she mumbles.

Nicola grabs her arm – Olivia can feel her fingers dig deep into her skin. 'Bad habits need to be broken.'

What the hell is that supposed to mean?

But Nicola lets it go. Instead she reaches over to the iPod, flicks through for a change of track and turns up the volume.

With just a few last minute touches to their clothing, some squirts of body spray and more of their favourite make-up; with some laughs over Nicola's outrageous new shoes, and a bit of posing, they're almost ready to make their grand entrance down the stairs. Jonty and his mate Adam are already downstairs having arrived just before her parents left. She can hear them setting up the speakers; jeering at each other, blasting out X-rated songs now that her parents have

6

finally gone.

Olivia checks the time on her phone and half hopes, half dreads the first ring of the doorbell. One thing's for sure: she could really do with their mate Ben being one of the first visitors. He can be relied on to get a party going. His cheery banter always eases even the most awkward of situations. Apart from the ones between her and Jonty. In fact, Ben is sometimes the reason for awkwardness there.

Two sharp raps on the bedroom door and Jonty walks in. He's wearing black jeans and a denim shirt. His skin is shiny and fresh and he's washed his hair. It makes him even more good-looking. He seems excited and edgy.

They smile at each other. She feels tense goosebumps rise on her neck.

'Ready?' She notices his glance linger on her vest top, but thankfully he doesn't say anything.

There's a brief wash of his eyes over Nicola.

Olivia sees Nicola put weight on her back foot like she's nervous or worried about something.

But now there's the clatter of voices down in the hallway. They're here! Olivia takes a deep breath, walks across the landing to Alice's room, pops her head round the door where she sees her sister sitting on her bed sorting through her gemstones. 'You OK there, Alice? I'll bring you up some pizza later.'

Alice nods happily. 'I'm fine.'

Olivia closes the door and grins over her shoulder at the waiting Nicola. 'Then let the party commence.'

7

She likes the sound of the words as they echo around her landing.

Two hours in and the party is full on.

Music blasts against walls, jars against pictures, rattles amongst glassware littered on surfaces. The quiet little semi-detached house has never known such force. It literally quivers.

People are strewn around the two reception rooms. Their skin, their hair, their clothes are bathed in the glow of a good time. Boys grabbing each other in the front room, slam-dancing and moshing. Girls bent double in the lounge, laugh-ing over phones, cracking up with drinks balanced in wavering hands. Couples with their fingers all over each other; in hair, in clothes, in mouths moist with drunken laugh-ter. The kitchen teems with conversation and raised voices. Hard to be heard over the music.

Tiles tacky underfoot. Walls with giant shadows. Ugly, looming figures throwing exaggerated profiles against low lights and candles. Scents of perfume, sweat, beer, cider and wine. And one of a strongly fragranced candle which burns by the side of the computer. Despite the warmth of tightly packed bodies, there are blasts of icy February air which cut at ankles as they dance around the kitchen. The back door bangs open and shut as people stumble into the dark chill of the garden to smoke.

From where Olivia's standing, against the sink, next to two friends who are definitely worse for wear, she thinks it's going well. She presses her fingers against the cool of the ceramic behind her. This is a good party. She can just feel it.

She watches Jonty over in the corner, talking with mates Adam and Durant, their profiles throwing laughter shapes against the wall. Jonty looks happy.

That's a relief. Don't want him angry, not tonight.

Ben's dancing with a circle of friends – mainly girls. He's the centre; their faces all turned towards him, laughing. Olivia smiles with pride. He's her best boy friend. Came into her life only last year but a fierce friend all the same. Back at the start of the last school year he wandered into her Science class, a cloud of shaggy hair, shining eyes and outrageous shoes. He sat beside Olivia as it was the only free stool. Within minutes he was re-threading her friendship bands and telling her that if she liked The Horrors' music, and judging by the graffiti on her Science folder she did, then she should really revisit some original stuff from the eighties.

By the end of the lesson they were mates. He even managed to finish her question on photosynthesis.

He's now a regular visitor to her house. A day rarely passes when they don't see or meet each other. Olivia's mum thinks the world of him and even Nicola seems happy to share the friendship, they get closer every day. He's easy company, makes few demands and has both girls laughing at things which didn't seem funny before. He even makes an effort with Alice, who's unusual – to say the least – and awkward with people. But somehow Ben sees through this. He is kind and gentle with her.

It's only Jonty who doesn't get Ben. But it's sort of understandable – before Ben came along Jonty was the only boy she spoke to. It must have been a shock for him to suddenly have to share her. Besides, they are poles apart. Ben's obsessed with music and fashion; Jonty couldn't care less. He hangs around in trackies and T-shirts and hates shopping with Olivia. Anyhow, Jonty doesn't have any money. He lives with his nan and uses any money he *does* have on his gym membership and protein shakes. Ben, on the other hand, works in a cafe on Saturdays and spends all his wages on clothes and music by Sunday.

Watching Ben now, in amongst all the dancers, she feels a rush of love for him; gratitude for his friendship. She grins to herself. Maybe it's the cider.

She can't see Nicola. Now she thinks about it, she hasn't seen her for a while. Not since the first half-hour when they'd started off the dancing. She hopes she's stopped worrying about her appearance. She's normally laughing and joking with Ben or Olivia. It's weird that she's not around.

Pouring herself some more cider Olivia thinks briefly about Alice too. Sighs. She'll go and check on her in a bit. In a while. When she's had this drink. Maybe take her some pizza later.

Ben grabs her by the wrist, his eyes creased with laughter. Pulls her from the sink and her two drunken friends. 'C'mon, dance to this. It's so good.'

She allows herself to be dragged into the circle of bodies, weaving and swaying and pounding in time to the music. The drink; the music; the voices around her; the shadows; the smells. She gets sucked in. Swirls around. A giant, laughter-

10

filled, cider-infused twist.

'Where's Jonty?' Ben's sweating. It glistens on his cheeks.

'Not sure.' She points at a boy in the corner, Ben's current love interest. 'I see Mark made it then?'

Ben shakes his head. 'I've gone off him. His toenails are a disgrace.' He pulls his mouth down. 'A disgusting old-man yellow.'

She rolls her eyes. 'You're so picky. And a bloody perfectionist.' She has to shout in his ear, it's so loud.

He slides his warm hands over hers. 'There's nothing wrong with high standards.' Lifts his chin like he does when he's trying to make a point. 'Something you could learn from.'

She frowns, turns her head and thinks about changing the subject. She's been down this road with Ben too often. Ben's voice is careful, close to her ear. 'Don't really get why you still see Jonty.'

Olivia sighs. She looks around her at the swaying dancers. She stands on the edge, half dancing, half not. 'Everyone says that. It's just . . . I've been with him for so long that I can't imagine what it'd be like without him.'

The music morphs into another song. Someone's slick mixing.

'No offence, Livvy, but isn't he kind of . . . possessive?' His voice gets louder in her ear, more insistent. 'He definitely bullies younger kids. I've seen that myself.' He pulls away to check her eyes. 'And doesn't his body obsession bore you to tears?'

'You don't know him like I do.' Even to Olivia this sounds

weak. But it's true. They've been seeing each other for six years now. Since year seven. Thank God Ben decides to let it go – like Nicola did earlier. A party isn't the place. Ben always seems to know when she's had enough. He steps back and gets in some serious shuffling. It makes her laugh. He pulls her in with him again.

'By the way, I checked on Alice earlier,' he shouts in her ear again. His words are hot on her cheek.

'Was she OK?'

He nods. 'Yeah, she's so cute! Told me all about her imaginary farm.'

Olivia winces. She presses her thumbs together. Her sister's had an imaginary farm for the past two years now. She has horses, pigs and dogs. All named after precious stones like malachite and amethyst. Nobody knows why. Nobody dares ask. She has massive tantrums if someone suggests they're not real. And she insists on telling people about it. Olivia shouts back. 'It's a bit weird, isn't it?'

Ben smiles, shrugs and shuffles some more. 'You should have known me as an eleven-year-old. I was an emotional nightmare. I burst into tears if anyone so much as looked at my Star Wars Lego. I was sure they wanted to sabotage it, or at least nick Yoda.'

Olivia cracks up at the thought, shoves him in the ribs. 'I bet.'

Twenty minutes later. Face glowing, beads of sweat on her top lip, she thinks there was something she had to do. Only her mind's not working any more. She's been drinking too quickly. Jonty won't be impressed if he realizes how drunk she is. All that's in her brain are images and ideas, flitting and skittering behind her eyes.

She's standing with Jonty surveying the kitchen. He has his arm around her shoulders, but he's talking to Adam. It's OK though. He's in a good mood. There's a smell of burning pizza. She doesn't remember putting one in the oven, but someone must've done: Sarah Harrison's taking bites of a limp, wet-looking triangle. The tomato makes orange stains at the corners of her mouth.

Jonty points to a large chocolate cake by the kettle. 'Who's that for?'

Olivia rolls her eyes. 'That's mine. Mum seems to think that even though my birthday isn't till Thursday, just the fact that we're having this party means we should have a cake.'

Jonty shakes his head and rolls his eyes. 'Nice.'

'Look, I'm just lucky she's not putting on jelly and ice cream as well.'

'What time are they staying out till?'

'It took all my negotiating skills to get them to stay out until midnight. But I wouldn't put it past them to be early. It's way past their bedtime.'

'And Alice?' Jonty narrows his eyes. He's not a big fan. Doesn't know how to deal with her.

'She's promised to stay in her room. I couldn't persuade Mum to take her with them because she's been ill.'

Sarah wipes her mouth with the back of her hand and comes over. 'Someone's locked in your bathroom upstairs.

Reckon you might have to call the fire brigade.' She raises her eyebrows and takes one last mouthful of pizza. 'I'll take photos. Firefighters are so hot!'

They laugh, just as the speakers fizz and die.

Jonty swears, leaps over to the corner and starts to fiddle with wires.

No one else seems that bothered. The low ceiling bounces voices around the room.

This is a good party. The noise reminds her of a school canteen. Only more glasses.

There's something she should be doing. She's certain. There's a blast and another fizz and suddenly the music returns. Jonty stands proud, waiting for someone to be grateful. There's a dutiful cheer, and he grins. Olivia finds herself dancing into the front room to celebrate. She's not sure how she got there although she can still feel the circle of Ben's fingers around her wrist, so she guesses he must have dragged her to dance again.

Her drink's on the mantelpiece above the fire.

Glancing at the hallway, through the door she sees smears of birthday cake on the laminate. The swirls remind her of her grandma's curtains.

There's something she has to do.

Jake Moon bangs on the downstairs toilet door, his hand covering his mouth. His body is folded in a retch.

Lorna Cole holds a pack of cigarettes in the air, glints at Olivia, jerks her eyes to the back door. Olivia smiles, thinks about going to join her. Only Jonty hates the smell . . . Maybe

14

just one . . .

A while later, back in the kitchen, she spots Lorna through the window, smoking and laughing in the garden with a cluster of friends. Their movement switches on next door's outside sensor light. The Greaslys will be going crazy. But right now she's too happy to care.

This is a good party!

Another drink, some pizza. And now she's remembered what she was meant to do: check on Alice. She'll be nice and take her a slice of pizza. And where the hell is Nicola?

Jake Moon seems to have stopped vomiting now. And his hand is in Alice's goldfish bowl. Water splashes over the pine dresser. Oversized thumbs chasing goldfish.

Someone – she's not sure of his name – is playing air guitar with her mum's leopard-skin patterned broom. Random. She chinks glasses with Will Child. 'Brilliant party, Olivia.'

She sees his tonsils when he laughs.

She smiles and smells burning pizza again.

It reminds her that she's getting pizza to take up to Alice.

She wishes she could find Nicola.

Sometime later, there's an ugly scorch mark in the evening where things start to go downhill. She's walking upstairs, a slice of pizza on a piece of kitchen roll in her left hand. The right one clings to the banister.

Hot hands appear at her shoulders.

'Where are you going with that?' Jonty.

'It's for Alice. I just thought I'd check on her.' Olivia is surprised how slurred her words sound as they echo up the stairwell.

They walk upstairs, Jonty's hands moving to her bum. At the top, before she can turn left, he presses her to the right, to her bedroom door. His fingers push the door handle down and she finds herself in her room. Pizza still in her hand.

It's cool and quiet and the break from the onslaught to her senses is a relief. Hers and Nicola's clothes are in piles all over the floor and she feels the crunch of a tube of mascara as it shatters underfoot.

Jonty has his hands all over her. He's sweating and fierce. 'I hate this top,' he says, lifting the strap.

She takes a breath, not liking the way he pulls. 'It's fine.'

He yanks her hair. Her head tilts back and she has to tiptoe. It hurts so her heart starts to rattle a faster beat.

'Everyone can see your bra.'

'Stop it, Jonty, you're hurting me!' She realizes he's quite drunk. Smears of moisture slide around her neck from his lips.

'All you've done is dance with that twat, Ben. What kind of girl are you to be dancing with him all the time?'

'He's a mate.'

'He's an idiot. And he's always with *my* girlfriend.'

Olivia swallows, which is hard with her neck at an angle. Her calves hurt. 'He's gay, Jonty. Gay. He's no more of a threat than Nicola.'

'He's such a twat. His shoes are stupid.'

He mumbles under her chin, his hand still pulling on her hair. Follicles scream at the top of her scalp. There's a taste of

16

panic on her tongue. The pizza has fallen on to the dirty carpet. She probably won't be able to give it to Alice now. She'll have to go and get another piece . . .

'Will Child couldn't keep his eyes off you.' His words are low in her neck.

She can't talk any more with her head pinned back like this. He shoves her then, so that her head cracks against the wardrobe door. It sounds loud in her head. She can feel the door vibrate behind her. But she knows she has to keep Jonty calm. There's a shake in her words.

'Will's girlfriend . . . was standing right next to him . . . when he was talking to me.' She gasps for breath. 'And you should like this top . . . because I bought it with that gift voucher you gave me last birthday.'

He stops what he's doing and lifts his head to look at her, releasing her hair a fraction. It's enough to be able to catch his eye.

Olivia is suddenly stone-cold sober. 'Thanks for sorting out the music by the way, Jonty. Everyone's going on about how good the tunes are.'

His dark eyes make slits. There are party sounds all around the house, only in this room it's deadly, horribly calm. She hears someone crying somewhere. There's a banging on a door. The music gets turned up. Happy screeches outside sift through the window. The music's so loud it's distorting the speakers.

Jonty turns his head to the door. 'Need to sort the speakers. They'll get knackered like that.' He releases her hair and his arm falls by his side. 'Um . . . you OK?'

She nods and lowers her eyes, folds her arms. She doesn't want him to see she's shaking.

He moves towards the doorway then stops. He turns his head. 'Look, I'm sorry. I don't know what came over me. It's just . . . sometimes I think you don't like me any more.' He puts his hand on her arm. It's OK, the anger's over, she can feel it in his fingers. They've got a nicer grip.

He smoothes her cheek with hot, trembling fingers. 'Are you really OK?'

She nods, not trusting any words, and tries a smile. It works – he believes her.

Jonty searches her face then kisses her quietly on her lips. 'I love you.'

Things feel nicer. Now she can start to calm down.

Standing in the darkness, surrounded by clothes and make-up, she watches her boyfriend leave the room. Olivia lifts herself up on to her tiptoes and then rocks back on to the balls of her feet, stretching her muscles. She feels strangely calm, considering. Her scalp is stinging like mad. She breathes out.

Remembers the pizza on the floor.

And then to her horror, in a split second, she senses a movement from under the quilt on her bed. Someone's in her room. And has seen everything.

'So tell me again why you got scared?'

Alice is massaging the dog, Sandy, frantically. Her back is

pressed against her radiator in her bedroom. The dog pants happily. She's been with Alice almost all of the night.

'Because I could hear someone sort of moaning in the bathroom and because some people knocked on my door. They laughed at me.'

Olivia pictures her sister on her carpet playing with her imaginary animals, scared of strangers wandering into her room looking for a bit of 'space'. She can imagine her alarm. Her sister's weirdness is seriously annoying.

'So you came to look for me?'

Alice nods, her fingers active and restless in Sandy's fur. 'Sort of. Only you said not to come downstairs, so I came to your bedroom. It's a terrible mess, by the way.'

Olivia shakes her head. Sometimes her sister does her head in. But she feels bad for being cross. She's only eleven, she has a lot to learn. 'There are a few more people than I thought were going to come. There are some gatecrashers.' She pulls a face. 'There's no need to tell Mum. I'll make sure everything's tidied up for when they get back.'

Olivia smiles. There's a small silence. The music volume downstairs subsides a fraction – so Jonty has obviously sorted the speakers. The front door is opening and closing – are people starting to drift home? There's still a low moaning coming from the bathroom.

She'd better check on whoever's in there before her parents get back.

She starts to stand up.

'Olivia?'

'Mmm?'

'Why is Jonty sometimes horrible to you? He banged you against the wardrobe. It was really horrid. Why do you let him?'

Olivia sighs – pulls fingers over her head. It's still sore. There lies the million-dollar question. Why does she let him? How has it got to this point? All this pinching? This hair-pulling? The odd kick in the shin? Why does she let it happen? If any of her friends knew, they'd tell her to dump him within seconds. Nobody would believe it anyhow. Sometimes Ben and Nicola give her weird looks when they're talking about Jonty, but most of her friends – and she has many – think she's got the perfect relationship. It would be shameful to have to admit that he's started doing this sort of thing.

So why is she still with him? Why didn't she drop him like a ton of bricks after that first pinch about eighteen months ago?

She swallows and fidgets under her sister's unwavering gaze. For an eleven-year-old, Alice is genius-clever. And even though she's seriously weird too, she won't take being treated like a little kid.

She tries to brighten her face, but it's difficult and she's not completely certain that she's convincing her sister. 'Oh, don't worry about that. I think he's a bit drunk. He's normally fine in the end.'

Alice nods, but her mouth doesn't look right.

There's a wail from the bathroom, then a bang.

Alice rolls her eyes. 'She's been doing that for a whole hour now. It's really getting on my nerves.'

'Probably someone who's drunk too much.' Olivia nods. 'I'll nip downstairs and get Jonty or Ben. Reckon we might have to break the lock if she doesn't stop making that noise.'

Alice's eyes light up with excitement. 'Really?'

Olivia smiles and reaches for the door handle. 'Yeah. We had to do that at Jodie Bradshaw's party. This boy got so drunk that he couldn't undo the lock.' She looks down at her sister who has started eating the piece of pizza from the floor.

'Look, Alice. About Jonty?' She meets her sister's eyes at last. 'I promise I won't let him be horrible any more.'

And there, in the middle of her seventeenth birthday party, with a groaning person locked in her bathroom and music still reverberating around the house, Olivia truly means it: Jonty Newman will never touch her like that again. And if he does – then that will be the end.

She has to get Ben. He's lying on the sofa downstairs staring with glazed eyes at two boys who are laughing over a picture on a phone. She's not sure of their names. She shakes his shoulder. 'Ben, I need you upstairs.'

He's sluggish and unwilling to tear his eyes away, but unsettled by her tone he sways into a standing position. 'What's up?'

'Someone's locked themselves in the bathroom.'

He takes a deep breath, 'OK.'

Olivia checks her phone nervously. 'Mum and Dad'll be back soon. C'mon.'

They make their way up the stairs. They stand by the bathroom door – there's another low moan. They look at each other.

'Who is it?'

Olivia shrugs. 'Dunno, but I've not seen Nicola in ages. I'm worried about her. I wonder if it's her.'

'Nicola, is that you?' Ben calls.

Another moan, almost a growl. Olivia's heart thuds. She sees Alice looking anxious through the open bedroom door.

'Nicola – can you open the door? Let me in babe.'

There's no reply.

'Nicola!' She raps sharply.

Still nothing apart from that low moaning again. It prickles the back of her neck.

'We're going to have to break in,' she mutters to Ben. Best not think about her parents.

Ben squares his shoulders and jerks his weight against the door. It doesn't budge. He shoves against the wood again and still it doesn't move. But the moaning has notched up a level. It's got to be Nicola behind the door. And Olivia is supposed to be her best friend. What on earth is she doing in there?

'Here, let me help,' she says.

'After three.'

Ben and Olivia heave their bodies against the door at the same time and at last there's a splintering sound. After their second thrust, the thin wooden panel breaks and the lock gives way. They jostle their way into the small, hot room and peer at the sight before them.

It's not one they're expecting.

It *is* Nicola in there. But not the Nicola they're used to seeing. This Nicola is bent over, her head and shoulders over the bath. Her bum high. Moaning *and* wailing now.

At first Olivia thinks she's being sick. Throwing up in the bath.

But like the growl earlier, there's something animal-like about her position. This is so much more than drunken vomiting.

Olivia kneels down next to the quivering figure. 'Nic . . . Nic, you OK?'

Nicola shakes her head. Her cheeks are flushed high and there's a slick of sweat on her skin. She turns to her oldest friend. 'It hurts. It feels like I'm dying.'

Olivia places her hand on the small of Nicola's hot back. They're both shaking now. 'Where, babe? Where does it hurt?'

It's really hot in the bathroom. Nicola grabs her stomach. And Olivia notices with another sharp heart-thud that there is a large dome-shaped bulge there. There's a strange wetness all around Nicola's legs too.

'Oh my God.' She mutters under her breath. 'You're—'

But she's interrupted by Ben. 'I think we need an ambulance,' he says. He's not slurring or swaying any more.

Olivia feels her eyes widen.

I can't believe this.

One hundred questions sprint through her mind, racing after each other, chasing their answers, weaving knots. How can this be? How can her best friend be pregnant without her

23

knowing? Did Nicola even know? How the hell can she be about to give birth in the bathroom on a bath mat which is still damp from the shower she'd taken just a few hours earlier? Why hadn't Nicola told her? She hadn't even realized she was having sex. She swallows that thought but still feels . . . betrayed. Then she feels guilty because here's Nicola on all fours against her bath, looking like she's about to die. In the end it doesn't matter who knew what. In the end it's not important. She shakes herself and turns to Ben. He's standing by the radiator looking confused and slightly green.

'Go and phone for one. You get better signal in the lounge. Tell them . . .' and here she grimaces and flicks her eyes over Nicola's bulge. 'Tell them she's having a baby. And Ben,' she yells as he's walking out the door, 'make sure Alice stays where she is.'

When Ben has bolted out of the bathroom, when she's sat back down next to her friend who appears momentarily free of pain, she slides her back against the side of the bath and looks at Nicola's face. Her mascara has run and there are lines of pain etched either side of her mouth. Her skin is a pasty shade of cream with a sheen of sweat covering every pore.

There's a silence as they look at each other. It's a long gaze which ends when tears well up in Nicola's eyes and spill out on to her cheeks. 'I'm so sorry, Livvy.'

'For what?' Olivia's not sure.

Nicola leans back on her heels. 'This—' But a dart of pain

24

breaks up her face and she lets out a screeching wail which sends shivers down Olivia's spine. This is for real. There's no getting away from it. She rubs Nicola's back which has reared up again.

'Ooow.' Nicola yells, and starts to sob.

What do I do? Olivia closes her eyes and wills the ambulance to arrive. She's not sure she can do this. She can't even watch *24 Hours in A&E* without squirming. To have the real thing going on right in front of her is suddenly terrifying. She feels completely helpless. What she thinks is a contraction subsides and Nicola slumps into a ball on the floor.

Olivia grabs a flannel from the corner of the sink and holds it under the cold tap. She squeezes out the water and mops her friend's exhausted face. She looks about twelve years old.

'How the hell did this happen?' Olivia whispers as she wipes her cheeks.

Nicola opens her eyes but doesn't look at Olivia. 'Oh God, I don't know.' Her voice is shaky and she squeezes her lips together in a grimace. 'I guess I was pretty stupid about nine months ago.'

'Why didn't you say?' More wiping.

Nicola shakes her head and curls around her bulge. 'Because I was ashamed, I suppose.' And here she at last looks up at Olivia, 'I didn't know I was pregnant, Livvy. Honest. I didn't know this was going to happen.' She closes her eyes as they both begin to feel another contraction developing at the very heart of Nicola's body. 'My periods have been messed up ever since I went on that diet. You know that.'

The last words are said in another animal screech as the pain fills her body like a bolt of lightning. Only this time there's something dark in Nicola's face. Something so dreadful that an electric shock of panic flicks through Olivia.

'Oh God. I feel like I want to . . . push.' Nicola's breath is stale and her gasps are short.

Olivia feels her heart hammering and her palms slime up with sweat. This can't be happening. Surely the ambulance will arrive any minute now? Surely she won't have to deliver her best friend's baby in the bathroom at her own birthday party?

A bang on the door makes her almost laugh with relief. She rushes to the door and throws it open expecting to see uniformed paramedics holding strange, useful instruments which will help Nicola in the nick of time.

Only it's not. Instead it's Jonty and Ben, their faces confused and, in Ben's case, pretty anxious. Jonty just looks curious and grabs on to the door to poke his head round. 'What's going on?' His voice is thick with drink. He's obviously just followed Ben upstairs.

Nicola's breathing and gasping gets louder.

Olivia doesn't know why but she doesn't want Jonty in the room. Even Ben might feel like an intruder. But she's going to have to take charge and she needs someone to help. 'Jonty, listen, can you do me a favour? Can you get rid of everyone?' She jerks her head behind her, towards her wailing best friend. 'I don't want the medics to walk through a party when they get here.' She glances at her phone. 'Oh God, my parents are going to be back any minute.'

Jonty screws up his face. 'What's the matter with her?' Olivia pushes hair from her eyes. 'She's having a baby.'

Jonty's eyes practically burn with disbelief. He takes a step back and his mouth clamps shut. There's something else then. Something dark and complicated going on behind his eyes. But right now Olivia can't think about him. He backs out of the bathroom, his face a crumple of confusion. 'How long did they say they'd be?' she asks Ben.

Ben actually gulps three times before he is able to speak. 'Ten minutes.'

Oh God. Olivia grabs him by the wrist. 'Then we might have to do this on our own,' she hisses. 'Nic says she feels it coming.'

Ben's eyes widen, but Olivia has to give him credit; he inhales quickly and enters the hot bathroom. The first thing he does is open the window.

With shaking hands Olivia grabs a towel and points to the wet flannel on the floor. 'Use that to cool her face.'

'OK.' Ben looks scared but sits on the edge of the bath and mops Nicola's forehead.

Steeling herself, Olivia moves towards her friend's legs. Her hands shake as she peels back the sopping leggings; as she loosens underwear; as she observes misshapes and swellings. 'Nic, I'm just going to . . . take a look.'

Where are the ambulance sirens when you need them? Nicola screams.

Ben's words are indecipherable but his tone is just right.

There is no more music seeping through the bathroom floor now. Just the front door opening and closing again, and a few angry voices. Olivia can see the weird ripple of contractions going through Nicola's muscles. And something like the top of a head starts to appear between her legs. Olivia sits on her haunches and watches. It's like she's in a daze. Paralysed to the spot. It is the scariest, most panicky thing to watch in the whole wide world. But totally, amazingly mesmerizing.

She strokes Nicola's back and hears herself saying nice things, telling her to keep going, keep pushing. All the while she's staring at the small, dark head nudging itself further and further into their lives.

Only once does she take her eyes off it. And here she meets Ben's frightened gaze, his eyes drenching hers with encouragement and perhaps a bit of pride.

In a dream, in a trance, in a kind of fog, a small pink shoulder forces its way out. Olivia moves closer; maybe she needs to support the head? It seems so much heavier and bigger than before, a warm, wet, living thing which fits perfectly in Olivia's palm. She can feel a pulse with her fingertips.

Incredible.

Nicola lets rip a howl which seems to come from every square inch of her body.

There is another sound then which will stay with Olivia for at least a decade to come: a wet, tearing sound as the whole body comes out.

And then there is a baby. *I'm holding a newborn baby.* A damp, warm, blood-stained, sticky thing, with a mouth which opens and closes like a goldfish.

But a baby all the same.

And a silence. An incredulous and hot silence in which Olivia looks at Ben who's looking at Nicola who's looking at the baby in Olivia's hands.

'Oh my God,' someone whispers.

'What is it?' Nicola whispers slumping into a heap on the floor.

'It's a baby, Nicola. A freakin' baby.' Olivia can't stop staring now. The shock of this warm, living creature in her hands is immense.

Ben giggles from the side of the bath then clamps his fingers over his mouth. He speaks through them. 'She means what sex is it?'

'Oh,' Olivia looks quickly, catching Ben's giggle, feeling embarrassed. 'It's a girl.'

Ben clears his throat and looks hesitantly at Nicola. 'Did you really not have any idea, babe?'

Nicola shakes her head from the floor, moans softly. She can't seem to speak.

'She just thought she was putting on weight again,' Olivia says. 'I can't believe this. I can't bloody believe it.' Now the baby is here, she feels her knees tremble. She has to prop herself against the radiator. The baby's not doing anything and its mother is in a crumpled up, silent heap on the floor. There's a rush of fear which rages behind Olivia's ears.

She looks at the still baby in her hands and then towards Ben. 'God, what do I do now?'

But before they can think much further, the door is pushed open and Olivia's mum is standing there, her face stern and lined, her mouth tight and strained. 'What the hell's going on, Livvy?'

Behind her is Jonty, his eyes wide and unbelieving, and then Olivia's dad.

A frightening weeping sound slides from Nicola's mouth and she shifts her legs awkwardly to hide herself. The room is suddenly full of her sobbing. It echoes around the tiles of the bathroom, bouncing off ceramic and enamel and glass.

The noise springs Olivia's mum into action. She takes a look at Nicola; at the baby in Olivia's arms which is still connected to Nicola by a cord; at the blood; at the mess; and at the shock in both Ben and Olivia's eyes and yells at the top of her voice. 'Get out. All of you. Go away.' She twists her hair from her eyes and looks at her daughter, then puts out her arms. 'Have you phoned for an ambulance?'

Olivia nods, hands the baby over. 'It's on its way.' She looks at the baby. 'She's too quiet, Mum. Aren't babies supposed to cry or something?'

The horror of what might be happening is suddenly too much. Her whole body starts to shake.

The next ten minutes flash by in a storm of activity.

There's another phone call to the hospital. The last remaining party stragglers are ejected from the house by Olivia's blustering dad. The bathroom door is slammed shut and the three remaining teenagers and the tall eleven-year-old girl hover on the landing. Alice clings to Olivia, her face upturned and questioning. Olivia's been told by her dad to look after her because this sort of thing freaks Alice out. No one says a word.

Olivia's dad stands at the front door, looking from his watch to the end of the road. Olivia can't help noticing how the soles of his shoes stick to the smears of birthday cake on the floor.

Minutes twist by. Minutes of confusing information weave around them. There are movements behind the bathroom door.

Olivia feels Jonty shift by her side. He seems just as shocked as them all. He swallows and she watches his Adam's apple wobble up and down his throat.

Ben is crouched down, his hands over his face. There's no question that he's sober now.

Alice whimpers under Olivia's arm.

Olivia finds herself stroking the soft strands of Alice's hair. This is unusual. Her sister wouldn't normally let this happen.

And then the strangest sound. A noise which hasn't been heard in this house for the last ten years: the small yowls of a baby.

Olivia feels a sigh rock from her lungs. It makes her wonder how long she's been holding her breath. 'Oh my God.'

Her mum calls sharply from the bathroom. 'Get me a fresh towel, Olivia.'

Olivia rushes to the airing cupboard, her hands shaking

amongst the warmth of the towels. The bathroom door is opened by the smallest crack and her mum's hand pokes through. Her fingers scream urgency.

Olivia shoves the towel into the hand and wilts back against Jonty, who folds his arms around her. He smells like he always does, of shower gel and body spray. It's nice.

The scream of a siren comes from the open front door. Blue flashing lights flicker against the walls. Olivia's dad straightens his back. Preparing to direct the paramedics.

The four figures on the landing move towards the walls. Space will be needed.

Words in the hallway. Quick, brisk information is passed from one male to another. There are nods of acknowledgement and terse mouths.

A blanket. A bag of equipment. Heavy breathing on the stairs. Walkie-talkie crackle attached to a chest.

Alice watches with wide eyes. Sandy strains to be let out from the bedroom. Everyone ignores her. So she scratches at the wood.

Ten more minutes of activity in the bathroom. Figures move in and out and up and down the stairs. No one notices the three teenagers and the eleven-year-old girl. Olivia's dad comes to join them. She's never seen him look so old.

And then, when Olivia has almost given up, when she's sure she can't stand up for another minute more, the bathroom door is suddenly opened so wide that they can all see into the bright light.

Jonty steps away, against the wall.

32

First Olivia's mum, with a grim smile. She nods at Olivia's dad. 'They're OK.'

Olivia closes her eyes for a couple of seconds.

Then Nicola herself. Slack-jawed, glazed pink cheeks. The softness in her face seems suddenly beautiful to Olivia. She's on a kind of stretcher with a thick blanket around her. A paramedic is helping her. And in her arms is the baby. Something Olivia can barely fathom. A curled up, scrunched up wisp of a thing which Nicola cradles as if she's clinging to life itself.

She smiles. She actually smiles. Sheepishly at Olivia. And Olivia smiles back.

And it's while she's smiling that she catches the quick, awkward glance flicked between Nicola and Jonty.

When they're gone, when they've left through the front door and the ambulance doors are crunched closed, Olivia blinks and feels a wave of fatigue.

'I think you'd better go.' Olivia's dad nods to the two boys whose arms are hanging by their sides in identical awkwardness.

Ben collects himself first. 'Um . . . do you want some help clearing up?'

Olivia's dad pulls his fingers through his hair. The lines at the side of his mouth are deep. He shakes his head. 'No. We'll leave it till the morning. I think we could all do with some sleep.'

Ben nods, and Jonty shrugs. 'If you're sure.'

Olivia's dad seems to want both boys out of the house. He

33

starts to usher Alice towards her bedroom. They're both nearly knocked over by the bounding dog as the door opens. Alice exclaims with pleasure. 'Sandy, you've been such a good girl.'

At the front door both boys linger. Ben shakes his head, 'I can't bloody believe it.'

Olivia allows herself a grin. 'Some birthday surprise.'

Jonty remains silent, his face still strained.

'What I don't understand is . . .' Olivia watches as Ben twists the latch to open the door, his face open, waiting, 'who the hell is the father?' Olivia's voice is tense. She can't get it out of her head. Nicola has not had a boyfriend for over a year. She'd assumed her friend was still a virgin. She remembers precisely the day when she'd told Nicola about her first time with Jonty. They'd been on the swings sucking ice pops, and Nicola's eyes had sparkled with interest when Olivia had told her everything. Isn't that what best friends did? It doesn't feel right that Nicola hadn't told her.

And then she can't help noticing how quickly Jonty rushes through the door. She watches the back of his head, remembering the odd look which passed between them as Nicola held the baby in her arms.

And suddenly she doesn't feel good. Blood rushes to her cheeks which makes her feel faint. She doesn't like the thought of the look. She doesn't like it one little bit.

Suddenly it feels, with this new and unexpected arrival, that nothing will ever be the same.

nicola

march

There's a sharp rap on Nicola's bedroom door. She winces and thinks of the sleeping baby. Her mum doesn't seem to have remembered. It's like she forgets on purpose sometimes. Her mum's head pokes through the gap between door and frame. The corners of her lips are turned down and her eyebrows are raised in disapproval. 'It's Alice. She's downstairs.'

Nicola, with effort, raises her head off the pillow. 'Can you send her up?'

Her mum looks around, frowning. 'Let's clear this up first.' Nicola's head flops back against the pillow, her mind dazzled by the stuff around her. She is confused.

How did this all happen?

She watches her mum moving around the room, opening curtains and sniffing the air. Pointedly opening the window. Her bedroom, the same one in which she played with a doll's house when she was five, with Barbies a year or so later, with an art set and easel when she was twelve years old and with her laptop and DVDs last month, is now given up totally to the huge collection of stuff that a baby seems to need.

There is a stack of nappies in the corner, spilling out of their plastic shrink-wrap. A cot, still in pieces, wedged against the wall, waiting for someone – God knows who – to put it together. A mobile with blue, stuffed whales tangled together is in its polythene bag, hanging off one of the cot posts. Triple packs of babygrows and vests are piled untidily on her chest of drawers. There's a plastic baby bath, a baby rocker, a sling for carrying the baby, which Nicola has no intention of wearing because it looks disgusting, and pots upon pots of

37

creams and potions and liquids. All in pastel colours. They're seriously beginning to do her head in.

Only five weeks ago she was getting all her clothes ready for Olivia's party and this room was like any of her school friends' rooms. Posters peeling off the walls, photos and pictures everywhere. Clumps of clothes (from her fat or thin wardrobe depending upon how her diet was going) crumpled on the floor. Make-up spilling out of handbags. A phone. An iPod. Headphones. Speakers. Perfume. Deodorant. Screwed up make-up wipes with mascara smears and foundation smudges. Crumpled tissues.

But now hardly any of these are left, just a few posters and photos. She can't remember the last time she used make-up. And what's the bloody point bothering about what clothes to wear when A: you won't be seeing anyone of interest, and B: the clothes don't suit you any more? Even from the fat wardrobe.

So everything's been scooped away. Cleared back into drawers and hung on to hangers, to keep the carpet clear for the trek from bed to Moses basket in the middle of the night, which happens every other hour. Five weeks ago, Nicola didn't know what a dawn chorus was. Now she hears the birds come to life outside her bedroom window every morning with a sense of doom that the night is almost over and she's had exactly two hours sleep.

She crumples her fists on her quilt. There are milk marks on her hoody and small splatters of an unidentifiable liquid, possibly baby sick, maybe more milk, on the thighs of her leggings. The same leggings that she's been wearing now for

38

the best part of a month.

She closes her eyes. Who bloody cares what's she's wearing? She's so tired she doesn't give a toss. The way she's feeling right now, she'd happily wander round in nothing but a sleeping bag, so long as it meant she could sleep when she wanted.

Her mum straightens her quilt cover, scowling.

A small whimper and a starfish flash of fingers coming from the Moses basket catches Nicola's eye. It makes her jump. She feels a cocktail of emotions tug at her insides, a mixture of fear and pride mingled with a horrible tiredness; it's as much as she can do to turn her head.

The baby. Eliza. The name chosen after a session on the internet with Ben because it means joyful. The most gorgeous curled up, pink creature you could ever imagine. Feather-soft. Papery, drawn-up thighs. Tiny shell fingernails. Delicate fingers which flash open and curl closed and move around even when she's asleep. She might play the piano when she's older.

But also the greediest guzzler of time and energy that can possibly exist. Nicola feels like a shell. An empty, sucked-out shell with nothing better to do than shift around listlessly, waiting for the noisy demands of this beautiful creature.

She's had so many people ask her how she feels, so many questions . . . Are you pleased you had her? Do you want to give her up for adoption? Can you cope? Are you getting enough sleep? Are you safe to look after her on your own? Have you got help at home? What about school? What about after school? What about your ambitions to work for Versace? Have you got enough money for nappies? Will you be applying for benefits? Where will she sleep? Are you sure you can cope? Are you sure you don't want to give her up for adoption? Where's the father?

Social workers, midwives, health visitors, teachers from her school. But she doesn't really know how to answer. How can she possibly describe the raw emotions drifting around?

That's why she spent so long in hospital. Nobody dared let her out. Nobody was prepared at home for a start. Her mum – and there's only her mum, her dad left when she was a baby – works as a dinner lady at the local primary school, and then helps out at the after-school club every day. She can't take time off work. She needs the money – more than ever now, as she's told Nicola five hundred and eighty times since Eliza's birth.

The message is loud and clear: there is no time or money for this baby.

Her mum, now satisfied with the quick tidy-up of her room, purses her lips and her eyebrows knot together. She nods to the stairs where Alice must be waiting. 'She's a bit strange, isn't she? And why does she keep coming? Why not Olivia?'

'Shh, Mum, she'll hear.' Nicola pulls lank hair off her face. *It's gross. I really need a shower.* 'She's sweet. She's just a bit interested at the moment. You know what she's like. Gets a bit obsessed with things . . . Anyway, she helps. She changed a nappy and helped with Eliza's bath yesterday. It's nice to have someone to talk to.' It sounds sad. She knows that. It's horrid and hurtful how almost everyone's abandoned her.

Her mum frowns at the doorway. 'But I don't understand why it's not Olivia . . .'

Nicola puts a nail between her teeth. Won't look at her mum. 'I'm sure she'll be here soon. She's . . . dead busy at the moment.'

There's a disbelieving, disapproving sniff from her mum before she goes downstairs to get Alice.

Alice stumbles into the room, red cheeks, scruffy hair and trousers which are too short. This girl has no idea about fashion but doesn't seem to care. She's an awkward, lanky, younger version of Olivia. She can't compare to her stylish sister who is always surrounded by friends. Besides, right now, in baggy, stained leggings, with not a friend in sight, Nicola's no style icon either. 'Hiya.'

'Hello.'

She goes straight to the Moses basket, head as close as she can get. Bum in the air. 'Hello, little baby.'

Nicola watches from her bed. She's such a funny kid. She's come most days since Nicola got home. Stayed for about an hour; got her fix of baby information like she was writing a childcare manual; played with Eliza like she would a puppy; introduced the baby to her imaginary animals, which Nicola doesn't really get; then taken herself off back home. No explanation, no talk of Olivia, no questions asked about where she's come from or who the father is. In a way, it's a breath of fresh air from the interrogations off all the teachers, doctors and social workers.

Surprising. She'd never really noticed Alice before all this.

Just seen her as Olivia's weird little sister.

She picks up the lukewarm bottle which has been sitting in her pillows for some time, lifts it towards Alice. 'Want to feed her? It's almost breakfast time.'

Alice swings round, a flush to her cheeks. 'Can I? Is that all right? I'll be gentle. Like you taught me.'

Nicola smiles again. Nods.

Sweet kid.

The second visitor of the day is Ben. Her mum does another roll of the eyes when she comes home from the shops.

'He's always bloody here. Is there something you're not telling me?'

Nicola sighs. She has deliberately not told anyone who the father is. She knows it's why Olivia hasn't returned any of her texts or why she hasn't been to see her or Eliza.

'Mum, he's gay!' She hisses through gritted teeth.

Nicola's mum just tuts and shrugs her shoulders. 'Wouldn't be the first gay dad. Besides it might just be a phase. Boys like that often sort themselves out.'

Nicola exhales. Her mum is *so* old-fashioned, *so* embarrassing and *so* wrong. But she doesn't have the energy to confront her. And in a way she might be right. There was a time, not so long ago, when even Nicola had her doubts about Ben. There's a memory to wince at. Nicola shakes her head at the thought. Doesn't want to go there. It's almost funny. Besides, surprisingly enough, her mum's eyes have moved to the Moses basket and Nicola detects a slight softening in her cheeks. 'Madam kept you up most of the night then?'

Nicola nods. 'She's quiet now though.'

This is the first time that her mum had shown interest. She can count on the fingers of one hand the number of times her mum has even looked at the baby.

Nicola swallows and allows a faint wisp of hope to slide up her throat. 'I think she might be starting to get used to the place.'

Her mum purses her lips. 'So you want this Ben up here?' She looks doubtfully around the room.

'Please.' Nicola nods.

Her mum sighs and stomps down the stairs.

A few seconds pass by before she hears Ben leaping up the stairs. Then he is striding into her room. He has his usual grin and something in a carrier bag. Nicola cannot begin to think how she could have coped without his visits. He is the one person in all this chaos who has made her feel vaguely normal. The one person who appears to have stuck by her. Everyone else, apart from Alice, has dumped her. Like she makes everyone feel awkward.

'How is she?' Ben whispers, peering over the Moses basket. 'The health visitor says that we should talk normally around her so that she gets used to sleeping with noise.' Nicola screws up her nose. 'But right now I'm just grateful that she'll sleep. I'm willing to live in a soundproof vacuum if it means I get four clear hours.'

Ben grins and turns back to her. 'Dig the leggings, by the way, Nic. You aiming for a tie-dye design?'

43

Nicola pulls a face and covers the stains with the quilt. 'What's in the bag?'

He sits at the foot of the bed on the floor and upturns the carrier. 'New mum treasure.'

Indeed, tumbling from the bag are two packets of strawberry laces, gummy bears, a three-pack of Creme Eggs, a chocolate frog and a large tub of luxury-looking bath gel with an exotic label.

Nicola smiles for the first time today. It feels stiff on her cheeks. 'Oh my God, Ben. This is brilliant.'

He smiles sheepishly. 'I thought you could have a long soak in the bath, eat Creme Eggs and strawberry laces while I sit in here and watch my favourite newborn. I might get some revision done if she'll let me.' He pats his backpack where she can just about see the corner of a textbook.

The thought of relaxing under warm bubbles is suddenly too much for her. And to both of their embarrassment, tears glow in her eyes. She brushes them away.

'That's so nice. What did I do to deserve you?'

He shrugs and lies back on the floor, his hands crossed behind his head. 'It's what you're going to do afterwards that I'm more interested in.'

Immediately she says. 'I'm not giving her up for adoption.' She hears her voice swell out of her control.

Ben sits up quickly, his face pale and shocked. 'I wouldn't suggest that, you idiot. Never. She's yours now.' He nods over to the Moses basket. 'And she belongs to you. You obviously love her. Anyway, I wouldn't let you. She's fast becoming my favourite person under a metre long.'

Tension slides out of the room as quickly as it filled it.

'What then?' Nicola sighs, still wary, her hand squeezing the bath gel.

Ben screws up his eyes. 'Just my little plan to get you out of here.'

Nicola's knees tremble slightly. She's not been out of the house since she got home from the hospital and the thought makes her feel physically sick.

An hour and a half later, Nicola stands at the front door. It has been a military-style operation getting Eliza ready for her first outing. Nicola doesn't know what the baby will need. Between them, she and Ben have bundled the drowsy baby into a padded babygrow made for outdoors. It had, along with most of her clothes, been donated by well-meaning services or friends of the family. Her mother had scowled at the packages as they'd arrived through the door. Nicola remembered feeling bewildered by how much stuff there was. She couldn't understand how a baby needed so many things. Only as they packed a bag with nappies and bottles, a changing mat and wet wipes, did she start to understand. With a baby you have to plan for every eventuality. Even Ben seemed taken aback.

'Does she really need all this stuff?' he asks now, his hand on the latch of the front door.

Nicola shrugs. 'I guess so. What if she gets hungry or cold or wet?'

Ben grins. 'I was only planning on going to the shops. Not the bloody Antarctic.'

Nicola finds herself laughing, close to hysteria, stuffing her fingers into her mouth.

'Jesus,' Ben giggles, opening the door. 'So much for spontaneity.'

They bump the buggy through the front door. A wheel catches on the door frame and Eliza jerks and blinks hurriedly in the daylight. Nicola squares her shoulders and grips on to the handles. She suddenly feels like she's a five-year-old all over again, pushing a doll's pram. Something catches in her throat as she senses the importance of the moment.

'I feel stupid,' she mutters.

'You don't look it. We should have a photo to mark the occasion.'

Nicola rolls her eyes and stands awkwardly as Ben snaps the moment with his phone. 'I should've changed my leggings.'

He smiles. 'As I say: tie-dye. You're making a fashion statement.'

They walk down the road self-consciously, side by side. Past the run down farm building which looks dark and damp. Through the alley, past the park, along the path towards the small parade of shops in the centre of the village. The wheels of the unused buggy give off squeaks of newness. More nervous giggles and then, as an old woman passes by, she glances at the buggy and her cheeks soften into a smile. She looks from the baby to Nicola, then back to the baby. 'Aah, a

46

newborn.'

A tinge of pride forms at the pit of her stomach. 'Yes, a newborn' Nicola says. *My newborn.*

The words surprise her. Catch her out. Astonishing to hear them on her tongue.

They try the newsagent first, tilting the buggy over the threshold, wary of the door frame this time. Mr Thomas stands behind the counter. He's been there all Nicola's life and she's never seen him anywhere else. It took her until she was six to work out that he even had legs. Today he stands with his hands on his hips and smiles encouragingly. 'Your baby, I hear?'

Nicola nods shyly. Blood floods to her cheeks. 'This is Eliza.'

Mr Thomas smiles again and bends over the counter. 'Welcome, Eliza.' He takes the three steps necessary to reach the chocolate gift shelf, selects a box of Roses and holds them out. 'Here – take this. May this be the first of many visits. I'm sure I'll get to know her well.'

Nicola swallows and accepts the box. She has always liked this man.

But it isn't all as straightforward. For a start they have to negotiate a bunch of kids on the corner by the postbox. Some straddling bikes, the handlebars at an angle, elbows locked into place. Two girls Nicola vaguely recognizes from the year below gawp wide-eyed at Nicola with the buggy. Staring silently at the cracks in the pavement, Nicola can virtually hear their thoughts. She knows they won't be nice.

And then the supermarket isn't so welcoming. Ben wants

an energy drink and a new lighter for his fast-growing nicotine addiction and Nicola wants to look at the birthday cards. She knows that she missed Olivia's actual birthday, what with Eliza's surprise arrival. She was going to buy a picture frame and fill it with photos of the two of them from all the years they've been best friends. She wonders now about using a belated card as some kind of peace offering. Her heart feels heavy with the thought.

She misses Olivia. Her oldest, most trusted friend, Olivia. A friend through thick and thin. She thinks of Olivia's chestnut hair, her blue eyes and the wide smile like a sunrise. And how she's not her friend any more. And unfortunately for Nicola, she has nobody to blame. Nobody, that is, apart from herself.

The aisles are small and crowded. It's difficult to negotiate a buggy around all the people. A haze of rain has begun to fall outside, so it feels like everyone has come into the shelter of the shop. Eliza seems distressed by the sudden commotion and starts to thrash her fists around. Her mouth opens and closes and Nicola recognizes the beginnings of a screaming fit. She feels the tension rise at the back of her throat. She doesn't want to deal with a crying newborn in front of all these people.

I can't do it.

Even in the privacy of her own bedroom it's hard. She jiggles the pushchair from side to side.

Ben's at the counter, scrutinizing the jewel colours. Only he can spend so long deciding on the colour of a lighter. She hisses through her teeth. 'Ben, I don't think she likes it in here.'

Eliza begins to mew softly and Nicola's backbone prickles. She can feel eyes burn into the back of her head. Strangers. Neighbours. Even the bloody postman who is buying a bag of frozen peas; it feels like they're all watching. All judging. All whispering behind fingers. She swears she hears someone tut. Swears the words 'benefit scroungers,' get tossed over the cereal shelf.

'Ben,' she insists, her breath coming fast like she's just run a lap of the school field. 'Hurry up.'

Ben eventually picks a yellow lighter. 'Chill, babe. It's pissing down out there. Stay in here a while.'

'No!' She feels her mouth twisting anxiously, 'I want to go.' She's certain she can hear two girls snigger by the bread as they turn to stare at her. Eliza begins to wail now.

She jerks the buggy so that it's facing the door, her knuckles white on the handles, her cheeks burning red. 'Well, I'm going anyhow.'

Ben hurriedly hands his money over, finally understanding her distress. He follows Nicola's hunched shoulders and lowered head.

'They'll be getting a flat from the council next, you watch.' A comment from near the vegetable shelves.

They spin round.

Ben lifts his middle finger and calmly says, 'Fuck off,' to the pair of middle-aged women with nothing better to do in life than to gossip and to judge. Their mouths are a perfect O-shape of shock.

'That'll give them something to really bitch about,' he

snorts as he rushes Nicola and the pram through the swish of the automatic doors and out into the rain. Outside she starts to laugh with him, her fingers easing on the buggy.

'Their faces!'

It is really raining now. Sheets of it splatter against cars; iridescent oily marks pattern up the pavement. People run down the high street with their necks bent low, their collars up, hoodies pulled tight. Only it's not easy to run with a buggy. Once more, Nicola's reminded of her dolls' pram – and the races that she and her friends used to have, back when she was a kid.

Eliza's wailing is high now. She doesn't like getting jostled and although she's not wet – the hood on the buggy is pretty good shelter – it can't be nice getting shunted about as Nicola and Ben battle through the rain.

The wheels splatter Nicola's leggings with dirty water. Ben gets splashed by a car and swears. But at least she's not getting stared at now. At least the rain is proving a distraction. No one takes any notice of a regular couple and a buggy, hurrying through the rain.

They get to the house just as the rain stops. It's as if some-one has turned off a hosepipe. For a few seconds the whole road seems to be silent, holding its breath. Even Eliza stops crying at the sudden change in sound.

They stand, bedraggled, at the garden gate. Ben's big hair and Nicola's fringe are plastered to their scalps in messy rat's tails. Their legs are filthy with streaks of dark water and their cheeks glisten with moisture. The baby whimpers quietly and Ben grins. 'Shall I take another photo now? Before and after?'

She kicks him in the shin and feels for her key.

The front door is flung open.

'Where the bloody hell have you been?' Nicola's mum glances between the two of them and down to the baby who's cooing quietly in the glistening sunshine.

Nicola's confused. She's surprised at her mum's concern. She's never been bothered about her whereabouts before; never been standing at the door watching the time. That particular anxious parent routine belongs to many of her friends; Olivia's mum being an extreme example. Nicola was the first to be allowed into town alone; the first to go for sleepovers; the first to catch buses and be out all day on her own. They'd never been a family where you had to be back for mealtimes. That kind of routine just didn't exist for Nicola and her mum.

So it's all the more shocking to see her mother at the door with a furrowed forehead now.

'Out. Down the shops.' Nicola's voice is surprisingly watery.

'In this weather? With a bloody newborn? What the hell were you thinking?'

She reaches for the buggy and starts to pull it in. It bashes against the door frame and the wheels make greasy marks on the hall floor. Nicola watches her mother scan her grand-daughter. *She's checking*, she thinks, *she's actually checking to see if she's OK.*

There's a swell of something in the back of her throat. She's not seen her mum look so concerned about the baby before.

Eliza's fine. She's not even damp. 'She'll catch a cold,' her mum says. 'She'll get a chill. How could you be so stupid to take her out in this?' She tugs at the zip under the soft folds of Eliza's chin. 'If she gets ill and it's your fault they'll take her away. Surely you know that? They're watching you like a hawk. Don't you know anything?'

Nicola gulps and pushes at her wet fringe. All the fun of the last five minutes disappears in a flash. 'I didn't think . . .'

Ben interrupts. 'When we left the house it wasn't raining, Mrs Taylor. We got caught in the rainstorm. It took us by surprise. But we made sure Eliza wasn't wet and we're going to change her clothes as soon as we get upstairs.' Nicola stares at the swirls on the carpet. She swallows a smile. Ben is so good at this stuff. He touches her mum's arm. 'I'm sorry if we worried you.'

As they move up the stairs, conscious of her mum's suspicious eyes on her back, it takes all of her strength not to let the swallowed smile burst out on to her face.

Perhaps going out was a good idea after all.

For them all.

With a towel in his hands after helping her with the baby, Ben speaks carefully.

'Have you had a chance to speak to Olivia yet?'

Nicola glances up at his still-damp face. She's changed into a pair of grey trackies but her hair is still plastered to her neck. She lowers her eyes, fiddling with the poppers on Eliza's pale-yellow babygrow. 'No. I think she's avoiding me.'

He sighs and attacks his hair and face with the towel. 'I'm sure she misses you.'

There's a lump at the back of her throat. 'And I miss her more than anything. I've texted her loads. But she's not replied.'

'I think you should try and see her face to face.'

She sighs, puts Eliza in her Moses basket. 'I slept with her boyfriend. Why the hell should she want to ever speak to me again?'

There's a large silence which fills the room. Like she's underwater.

'And you wanted to . . . ? I mean, he didn't force himself on you or anything?'

Her mouth flops open. That he could even think this. And the shame. The pure, horrid shame. She drops her head. Whispers so that she feels him watching carefully to understand her. 'I wanted it as much as him.' She squeezes her fingers. 'I'm as much to blame as him.'

Another silence washes over the bedroom. It's true. Why would Olivia ever forgive her? There's a sigh from Eliza and her fingers flash wide. 'I think she wants her bottle,' Nicola says. 'I'll go and warm one up.' She walks towards the door.

'I think she's split up with Jonty.'

Nicola stops, holding on to the door handle. Her fingers are white.

53

'How do you know?'

'Cos she's all on her own at school these days. She looks so . . . lonely. So sad.' He gazes at her. 'Why'd you do it, Nic? Why did you sleep with him?'

Nicola stands still; just a quiver in her lower leg. She looks away. There are no answers, at least none she can give right now. 'I won't be a minute. You OK with a hungry baby?'

He slides a look at Eliza, lying in her Moses basket. Shrugs. 'If she's anything like her mother, then she's worth it, even if she's screaming her head off.'

When he's gone and she's left alone with a sleeping baby, when her mother has left for work, Nicola lies back into her position on her pillows and sighs. She thinks of Olivia. She thinks of Jonty.

How can she explain what she did? How can she love Olivia so much and yet betray her so badly? She shudders at the thought. It all seems years ago now. She was a different person. She doesn't really know the answer herself. But she knows for a fact that it's almost as if liking Olivia so much is part of the problem. Olivia has everything. A family; a fit boyfriend; friends; a generous nature; even a quirky sister. Nicola wanted to be a part of it. Compared to her friend she has none of this. An only child with a mother who scowls her way through life, who concentrates hard on 'getting through'. She wanted more. She wanted some of the attention, some of the buzz which always seemed to be surrounding Olivia.

*

A couple of weeks later Nicola decides to go out again. On her own this time. It's a Tuesday. Her mum's at work and she's pretty sure that she won't see any of her previous so-called friends because they'll all be in school now. She misses school. She doesn't mind admitting it. Misses the friends, misses the banter, even misses the work, especially Textiles and Graphics. She makes the effort. She dresses Eliza, changes into some loose-fitting jeans – at last she can fit into something other than leggings – and prepares the buggy.

It's a sunny March day. Gusts of wind, but no sign of rain this time. She checks Eliza for the umpteenth time and pushes the buggy down the front path.

It's all right.

She goes into the library where the librarian gives her a membership form for Eliza to join. She tells her about a monthly storytelling event which she and Eliza would be very welcome at, where she'd meet other young mums and perhaps make a few friends. Nicola even takes out a couple of board books because the librarian says it's never too early to start a baby's enjoyment of reading.

She places them in the basket underneath the buggy and tries hard to swallow the feeling that she's playing at being a mum.

She buys crisps and nappies in the supermarket. She'd like to buy the magazine she used to get and a pack of Oreos. But she can't afford it now. Not now she has to buy nappies and milk and baby clothes. She avoids the stares of a spiteful shop assistant; instead she uses the till operated by a teenage boy with pimples on his chin, who doesn't give Nicola so much as a glance.

She even goes to the greengrocer to buy apples.

It's good to be out in the fresh air. And Eliza's a dream. She gurgles and murmurs in the bright sunshine. Her cheeks look pink in this light. Pink and healthy.

But when she's in the chemist she gets a surprise. When the thing that wasn't meant to happen happens.

Nicola's scanning the shelf of baby wipes and nappy sacks when she catches a familiar frame in the corner of her eye. There's nothing she can do. She and Eliza would make too much of a commotion if they tried to hide. She can't slip anywhere with a great big buggy.

So she just stands there. Like an idiot.

Olivia stands there too. They glance at each other and Nicola sees a tight smile reach the corner of Olivia's lips – it's not her usual warm smile.

'Hello,' Nicola says shyly. She can feel her heart battering at her ribs. It's horrible being scared around her oldest friend.

Olivia nods, fiddles with a bottle of conditioner. 'Hello.' She seems a bit thinner and her hair has been cut short.

They stare at each other until Olivia sighs. She shakes her head and closes her eyes.

Someone sneezes in the queue by the counter. Nicola thinks about pushing the buggy out of the shop. Battering people as she goes. Escaping. Anything other than standing stupidly like this.

Eventually Olivia speaks. 'Well this isn't awkward.'

This makes Nicola smile. Olivia's always been able to do this. There's something about her which makes you feel at ease, even when you've done something as stupid as sleeping with her boyfriend. It makes Nicola realize again how amazing Olivia is. How much she's missed her. There's a small sob threatening at the back of her throat.

Eliza gurgles some more and they both look at the pink-cheeked baby who squirms happily. Nicola jiggles the buggy.

'This is Eliza.'

Olivia crouches into Eliza's eyeline. 'Oh God,' she brushes her hand over the blanket on Eliza's legs.

Nicola holds her breath.

'She's . . . gorgeous. She really, really is.'

'Thanks.'

'Just like her mum.' And then Olivia lifts up her head and says what Nicola feels to be the bravest four words in the entire universe. 'Not like her dad.'

So that's it then. Just as she'd thought. Olivia knows all the facts. Either Ben must have told her or she worked it out herself. It isn't a nice feeling.

'A little bird told me that you've split up with him.'

Olivia gets up. One of her knees clicks. Her face is blank but her eyes are honest. 'It's sort of on and off at the moment. It's not quite final yet.' She takes a deep breath, tilts her head. 'How is Ben? I hope he's OK. I miss him.'

Nicola trembles happily when she thinks of him. 'He's been brilliant. So nice. He's really good with Eliza.' She puts her head to one side like Olivia. 'Why don't you see him any more? He wouldn't tell me.'

Olivia pulls a face. She shrugs. 'I don't think he approves of my choices.'

'He loves you, Olivia. He's as confused as us all. It's sad that you aren't friends. It's sad that we aren't friends.'

The conversation has become too heavy too quickly. Nicola clings on to the buggy handles. Olivia twists the cap of the conditioner. They look at each other, and then look away. A homeless man comes into the shop; he carries three bulging bin bags. The pharmacist behind the counter looks nervous.

Olivia drums her fingers on the bottle. 'Um, I'd better go. Got Biology in ten minutes.'

Nicola nods.

Olivia trills a hand towards Eliza. 'Bye Eliza.' And she's gone, leaving a scent of honey and her favourite body spray so wonderfully familiar that it makes Nicola's throat ache.

When Alice next comes over, Nicola decides to ask. They're sitting at the bottom of the bed changing Eliza out of her baby-grow and into a cute pair of donated jeans. Alice likes doing this sort of stuff.

Nicola is careful. 'Um, how's Olivia?'

Alice looks up, then back down. Her eyes flash for a brief second. She fiddles with the baby jeans. 'She's all right, thanks.'

'Does she still have everyone coming round to see her?' Alice shakes her head. 'Jonty's stopped. It wasn't very nice when he did come. They kept crying. The horses used to hate it. They were so noisy.'

She puts a lock of hair behind her ear. Squeezes her eyebrows together. 'Mum says they have officially split up now. But she said to Dad that she doesn't know why.'

Alice's hoodie is too short for her. It makes her arms look long and awkward. She eyes a feeding bottle hopefully. Nicola knows that she loves feeding Eliza. She's actually quite good at it now.

'Did they—'

But Alice has more words to come. Her chest is bursting with them. 'And Ben doesn't come round any more either. He got cross one night. I was supposed to be asleep but I could hear everything. He said to her that sometimes you had to be a bigger person. Which I didn't really understand. And that best friends mean the world. But I didn't understand that either. Besides, my animals were so noisy that night, it was hard to hear everything.'

Nicola feels a small hopeful jolt in her stomach. It's soft and glowing. Ben standing up for her? It's lovely. Saying nice things about her to Olivia.

She lets Alice pull up the jeans over Eliza's little nappy. Eliza looks so cute it's hard for Nicola to take her eyes off her. But then she thinks of her best ever friend, and the betrayal. She finds herself grimacing. 'I bet she's lonely.'

Alice nods as she pulls at the baby jeans. 'Yes. It's very quiet in the house. No you, no Jonty and now no Ben.'

'Poor Olivia.'

Eliza starts to grizzle.

*

59

'You can go out if you like.'

'What?'

Nicola eyes her mum suspiciously. She's just spent the last hour wrestling with a grouchy Eliza. Bathing her, feeding her the bedtime bottle and trying to get her to sleep. It's eight o'clock. *Eastenders* is on. Her mum's legs are on the coffee table and she has a cup of steaming liquid in her right hand. She looks grey and tired. This week the school has had an Ofsted inspection and Nicola knows how much pressure her mum has been under.

Nicola can't quite believe that her mum has just said this. It's hard not to sound shocked. 'What?' she says again.

Her mum repeats the words, her eyes still on the screen, her head resting on a fading purple cushion. 'You can go out if you want to.'

Nicola gives in to a gape. 'Where would I go? You mean without Eliza?'

Her mum gives a harsh bark of laughter. It shakes her cup of tea. 'Wherever you like, I don't know. To Olivia's or that bloody gay boy's. And yes, I mean without Eliza.'

Her mum is a constant surprise. Nicola has never dared ask. She's never once requested help. Never once asked if she'd take Eliza for a second. Knows only too well how she'd say something along the lines of, 'She's yours for life now. She's your choice. You gave up that kind of life when you decided to keep her.' She's mentioned too many times how the father needs to cough up some money. How he's got off 'scot-free'. Nicola knows her mum too well. Her mum can be the scariest,

60

most scornful, saddest person alive.

Nicola blinks, unconvinced at the state of her clothes, the state of her greasy hair.

She's almost breathless at the thought of seeing Olivia. 'I'll only be an hour. Two at the most. I could be home before ten. Before she needs her late-night bottle.'

Her mum nods. Her eyes still on the screen. 'It's been seven weeks now. I've been impressed.'

Nicola feels her jaw drop again. She knows how difficult these words must be.

Before her mum can change her mind she finds herself rushing to the mirror in the hallway. Grabs her mum's hair-brush from the windowsill, even pinches some mascara. She could do with her phone and her purse, but they're in her bedroom and nothing on earth would make her disturb the peace behind her bedroom door.

She pulls the brush through her hair. *Please be home, Olivia. Please be home.*

Nerves like a siren, Nicola battles down the road. After seven weeks with a baby attached, she feels strange. As if she's missing a limb. No phone and no money, she walks quickly along the pavement which she's used since she was seven years old. Past the hawthorn hedge, along the parade of shops now empty except for the supermarket, which pours a blue light on the stretch of road. Then around the corner of the cul-de-sac where Olivia lives. One, two, three houses, and then Olivia's, lit up like a Christmas tree. Four windows of orange light and an outside lamp.

She stands at the front door. Holds her breath, fills her lungs with anxious oxygen. And before she can think about it she presses the doorbell. Her finger wobbles.

Thirty seconds or so pass in which she sees shadows and hears laughter from behind the frosted glass of the front door. This house is hardly ever silent. It feels like there is almost always life inside it. It's a stark contrast to the hush of her own.

Olivia's dad opens the door. The smile which cracks his face heartens Nicola. 'Hello stranger,' he says, his eyes sparkling. 'How's my favourite crazy teenager?'

No mention, she notices, of the last time she was here. She gulps down a strange sensation when she realizes that she's about to enter the house where she gave birth to Eliza.

Olivia's mum peers over her husband's shoulder. She's smiling, but Nicola can feel an awkwardness rock under her ribs when she remembers the last time that they met. 'How are you, sweetheart?' She looks past Nicola as if to enquire where the baby might be. 'How's the little one?'

'She's fine. Thanks, by the way . . . for what you did.'

Olivia's mum half smiles in a way which makes Nicola think of Olivia. 'That's OK. You'll have to bring her over sometime. I'd love to meet her properly.'

Nicola flexes her foot against the front step. 'I will do. One day, when she's not asleep. Is Olivia in?'

Olivia's dad widens the door. 'Sure. She's in her bedroom.' He nods at the stairs. 'Go on up.'

It feels odd walking up the stairs. She hasn't done this for

62

seven weeks. Is it weird to miss stairs?

At the top, she forces herself to knock and turn the handle on Olivia's bedroom door, next to the bathroom. The bathroom where her baby was born. She pushes the thought to one side. If she doesn't do it now then she might just walk right back down the stairs and forget about the whole exercise. Possibly for ever.

She pokes her head around the door and fixes a smile upon her lips. 'Hi.'

Olivia's on the floor. Her back against the radiator, her laptop on her knees. A glow of unflattering blue light patterns her face. The familiar smell of Olivia's room fills Nicola's lungs like honey and freshly baked biscuits. She could breathe it in for ever.

Unsure of her welcome, she loiters in the doorway.

Olivia shifts the laptop off her knees, straightening her legs as she does so. 'Oh, hi.'

'Can I come in? Are you busy?'

Flickers of emotion pass over Olivia's eyes. Nicola wishes she could read them. But they're too quick and the light isn't that good.

'No. I'm OK. Come in.' She nods to the bed for Nicola to sit. There are several seconds of agony between them. Above everything, Nicola regrets this. Never, in all their years of friendship, has there been awkwardness like this.

She can hear Alice speaking to her animals across the landing and some sounds of the TV downstairs. She kneads the quilt on the bed with her fists. Her hair falls over her cheeks.

There are hundreds of words to speak, but she can't manage to say any of them.

She nods at the doorway. 'Your sister has been coming over.'

Olivia rolls her eyes. 'Yeah. Is she making a nuisance of herself?' Her hands move about nervously.

There's another silence and then Nicola shrugs. 'No, she's great. She's actually a big help.'

Olivia nods and stares into the corner of the room. 'That's good.'

Nicola feels like her throat is clogged up with cotton wool, but she knows she has to say it. Say the words which she'd do anything never to have to speak.

She coughs.

She fiddles with the duvet cover. One that she's never seen before.

It's hard to breathe.

'I'm sorry, Livvy.' They come out croaky. She wonders if she might cry. There are certainly tears blocking up behind her eyes and her nose and her mouth.

Nothing. Just a nod. Looking closely, she can see grey smudges under Olivia's eyes. She looks scrawny and drawn, hunched up by the radiator.

'I'm really sorry to have screwed you over like I did.' Olivia nods again, gazing into the distance behind Nicola's left shoulder. 'I wondered . . .'

A sob surprises Nicola. It comes from her throat. 'It was the most stupid thing I ever did. I don't know what I was thinking.'

Olivia still doesn't look at her but her voice is suddenly direct. The words are strong.

'He said it was only the once. But I've been thinking about it. I've been thinking about it a lot. And I'm not that sure any more. Can you tell me? Can you tell me how many times you had sex with my boyfriend?'

All of a sudden the tears escape. They stream from Nicola's eyes, sliding over the contours of her cheeks and chin, dripping on her jeans, making dark, unhappy stains. She brushes them away but still they come. Her nose drips and she can taste the salt, even though her lips are clamped shut. Her throat feels wide and hot.

She stops brushing the tears. There doesn't seem any point as they just keep coming. She's not cried like this for a long, long time and it seems like there is a month's worth of mucus fighting to escape. The tears drip on to the back of her hand. Strands of her hair become damp and wavy around her sodden skin.

Olivia waits by the radiator, her face strangely impassive. Nicola knows that she is waiting for the answer.

A minute creeps by. A minute of tears and moisture and guilt. Olivia's fingers weave slowly together. Nicola's get wetter.

How could she have been so stupid? How could she have done the only thing she could have done to jeopardize a friendship which meant the world? And how can she explain the thrill of it? Nothing like that ever happens to her. Nothing.

65

She'd been at Joe Peterson's party, having a breather in a bedroom. She's always liked to walk around other people's houses. Getting an idea of how they live. It's probably because her own house is so quiet. So boring. So she wandered upstairs into Joe's bedroom, full of football trophies and posters; perched herself on his boy-smelling bed and looked around. She felt particularly fat that night. Her jeans seemed tight on her waist and she pictured the unpleasant layer of white fat spilling over the denim underneath her tunic.

And then Jonty turned up. Thinking about it now, she's sure he followed her up the stairs. She can't be sure because he didn't say very much, but even now she can feel the electric current fizzing between them in that room.

He stood, legs wide apart, planted in the centre of the bedroom, his head to one side. 'I just . . .' he uttered, before moving forward to kiss her. Suddenly she didn't think about her fat any more, suddenly it didn't seem to matter. All she felt was this boy kissing her and kissing her like nothing else seemed to be an issue. The kiss moved from her lips to her neck; from her neck to beneath her clothes.

And there she'd lain, bewildered and excited, unpeeled and shocked.

Kissing Olivia's boyfriend on Joe Peterson's bed.

Jonty wasn't saying anything, but he was doing a hell of a lot.

When it was finished he'd lain on top of her for just a couple of seconds, then he rolled over and began adjusting his jeans. He was awkward. So was she. He wouldn't look her in the eye.

She could have done with that.

He straightened himself and glanced at the door. 'I'd better . . .' He nodded downstairs, where Olivia was. Olivia had probably not even noticed. Too busy dancing and laughing and chatting with the crowd of people who seemed to follow her wherever she went. It was sometimes annoying to see. She looked especially gorgeous that night. A dress from River Island, high heels which thinned her legs and accentuated her calves. She probably didn't even notice Jonty or Nicola's absence. That was part of the problem.

Nicola glanced at the clock radio by the side of Joe's bed. Fifteen minutes. *Fifteen minutes.* That was all it had been. But it had felt like fifteen years. The shift inside her was immense. She'd only ever done it once before. An experiment in her bedroom, which had gone embarrassingly wrong. Something she didn't want to think about. But this . . . this, with Jonty. This was very different.

But then it happened again. Two days later, while walking a dog for a neighbour.

In a field. By a hedge.

And then another time, barely a week later; at a village wedding reception, behind the community centre on the fire escape steps.

It was like they couldn't get enough of each other. It was wildly exciting. Thrilling. Her stomach felt like it was on fire. Her mouth and neck burnt all the time. There was a permanent ringing in her ears. She felt alive. She felt pretty . . . and yes, she felt guilty. And this just made it all the more exciting.

The guilt was somehow mixed up with the pretty feeling. *This must be how it feels to be Olivia,* she'd thought. This was how it must be for every other non-fat person in the universe.

The last time was in Olivia's bedroom. That was reckless. They had been waiting for her to come back after picking up her sister.

'Can you amuse yourselves for a bit while I go and get Alice? I'll only be half an hour.'

She saw Jonty's eyes; how they narrowed and fluttered at the word 'amuse'. She knew exactly what he was thinking.

Only Olivia came home sooner that they thought. They heard the front door open and the girls' innocent voices as they skipped upstairs. The twisting of clothes, the breathless panic when they realized what they had done. It wasn't exciting this time. Instead, it was frightening and heavy and riddled with guilt.

'No more,' she said swiftly as Jonty did up his jeans. And Jonty nodded with her.

And that was that.

Flushed, and packed full of bleak, heavy guilt, Nicola met the eyes of her best ever friend when she came through the door and she vowed that no matter what happened, however much she felt like it, she would never, ever do that thing again. Her friendship with Olivia meant too much. And judging by Jonty's unease standing at the windowsill, he felt the same.

Sighing, Olivia reaches for a box of tissues. She's been waiting quite a while. She tosses them gently on to the bed next to

Nicola. 'Here,' she says.

It's as if she knows.

So Nicola says the necessary words. Her friend, if nothing else, deserves some honesty. 'It was four times.'

'Oh.' Olivia studies her fingers furiously.

'So sorry.' Nicola whispers, pulling tissue after tissue after tissue from the box. She'll empty it in seconds.

Olivia has a neat parting in her chestnut hair, a pale line running from her crown to her fringe. It's like everything about her: smart, orderly, organized.

'I think I might have been jealous.'

Olivia nods. Glances up. Chews on a nail. 'I can't say I understand it. It's so cruel. To do it to a friend. To your oldest friend.' Her voice wobbles and she stares at the chewed nail. 'Um . . . but can I ask? Have you told him . . . Jonty, I mean? Have you told him he's the father?'

Nicola blows her nose.

Her turn to bite a nail. She thinks about the question. Attempts to remember the phone call that she'd made and tried to blank from her memory for weeks now.

Hospital had been difficult. She was sick of seeing people come and go with newborn babies which had been planned for and celebrated. Where the parents cooed and gushed over the tiny forms swaddled in brightly coloured blankets. Nicola had to make do with the faded threadbare efforts which the hospital supplied. She was sick of grandparents, siblings, dads and friends of these tiny creatures who had visited the

69

ward, laden with flowers and silver balloons. Nicola had no one. Nobody visited Eliza. No one had expected her and no one welcomed her into the world. Except perhaps the stream of visitors from the authorities who asked a long list of frightening questions and hardly ever looked at the baby.

That's not quite true. Ben came twice. Nicola could have kissed him there and then when the first thing he did was reach out to Eliza, let her pearl fingers clutch on to his little finger with her strong grip. He brought her a small purple donkey, which he placed in the corner of the Perspex cot.

Two of the mothers in the ward smiled indulgently at him; they nodded their approval and asked over the heads of their brightly-coloured-blanketed babies if he was the dad. That made him laugh.

The only other visitor who didn't have a badge to state their employment was Nicola's mother. And a tower of strength she was not.

In fact, it took ages for Nicola's mum to drag herself away from the ward doorway. She stood with her arms folded and her lips tight and thin. Just a line where a smile should have been. A thin, straight, grey line which spoke volumes. Without glancing in the baby's direction she jabbed with her words.

'What the hell are we expected to do now?'

Without laying eyes on Eliza, 'And where's the bloody father?'

She continued, jabbing with her finger into the silent air of the listening ward. 'I'll tell you where he is. He's off scot-bloody-free. That's where he is.'

Nicola had looked around, embarrassed at the faces of all the other new mums.

And she pushed all thoughts of Jonty Newman to one side.

But, drained and tearful, she'd eventually plucked up the courage to phone him.

She could hardly manage the words.

It was late at night and she didn't want to disturb the other women in the ward, or their babies. So she spoke softly once he answered after the eighth ring. Her hands shook.

Despite everything – despite their kisses; despite their links with Olivia; despite their knowledge of each other's bodies and scents – they hadn't really spoken very much.

'What do you want?' he answered.

Silence as she caught her breath. 'She's yours, Jonty.'

A full ten seconds of pounding silence. She wondered if he was still there.

And then four chilling words that stabbed at Nicola under her sheet in the warmth of the maternity ward. 'You are a slag.'

He'd hung up then. And the words rang in her ears for the rest of the night.

She was never going to contact him again. Whatever happened, she knew she was on her own.

Nicola looks at her friend's face. Her paleness, her deep eyes, the hair which she's pushed back behind her ears.

She nods. 'Yeah, I told him.' She clears her throat. 'He wasn't very impressed.'

Olivia pulls the sides of her mouth down and nods. Inhales. 'Well, Nic, I reckon you might just have done me a favour. If nothing else you made me see the light.' She draws her knees up and holds Nicola's eyes. 'Tell me, how are you doing for money?'

Nicola balls the tissue in her hand. 'Oh, you know, I've had to fill in about fifty million forms for this benefit and that benefit. There are even a few charities involved. I've been assigned a temporary social worker, which is weird. She's been good though. Lets me know what I'm entitled to and stuff. But it looks like as soon as Eliza's old enough I'll have to get some work. Cos as my mum keeps telling me, there's not enough money coming in, even with the benefits. So I won't be going to uni, like you. And I'll be lucky if I work for New Look. Versace's definitely not going to happen now.'

Olivia pays attention, her head to one side. Nicola is reminded of how good she is at listening. She nods. 'And Jonty pays nothing?'

Nicola shakes her head. 'My mum keeps going on and on about it. I haven't told her it's Jonty,' she adds in a rush. 'I haven't told anyone.'

Olivia shuffles forward on her knees and then reaches for Nicola's fingers. Both sets of hands are warm and damp. She winces. 'Well, Nicola Taylor. I might not ever be able to forgive you. I might never understand.' She draws her hand away and bites her nail again. 'But I *do* think I can help you. Whatever happens, Jonty needs to take responsibility for his actions. And I'm going to make sure he does.'

72

Not completely sure what Olivia means, but grateful all the same, Nicola tries a small smile. It hovers. 'You will?'

Olivia nods. Squeezes Nicola's fingers. 'I will.' There's a slight return of the smile. 'And you know what?'

Nicola widens her eyes in a question.

'. . . I might actually enjoy it.'

Nicola bites her lip, hardly daring to admit the rush of relief. It feels like she's getting her friend back.

Eliza won't settle. Almost as soon as Nicola arrives home from Olivia's she begins to grizzle. Her knees draw up against her tummy and her face becomes pinker and pinker as her temper gets more frantic.

Nicola tries everything. She remembers how the health visitor has told her to run through the checklist. Is she hungry? Does she need changing? Is she too hot? Is she too cold? Is she wet? Does she just need a cuddle?

None of this works. In fact, with all the checking and the manhandling Eliza just seems to get more and more upset. Nicola's scared. She's at her wits' end. It is nearly midnight and the crying has not shown any sign of stopping. She's conscious of her mum in the next bedroom. The impatient knocking on the wall hasn't started yet but she's sure it won't be long before it does. It is a school night after all, and no one with any sense of hearing could sleep through the racket coming from this small bundle of fury in Nicola's arms.

Sweat spreads across her back. Prickles of anxiety encase her throat. She can't stop her baby crying. She must be

73

rubbish. What made her think that she could do this?

She paces with Eliza from the Moses basket to the window, from the window to the bed. She swaps the screaming baby from her left shoulder to her right. She rocks her, she sings to her, she lies her down, she picks her up again. Eliza just won't stop the screams or the wailing. Her little face is purple with rage and her fists clench in anger.

Nicola suddenly misses the hospital. It was very difficult in there but at least there were nurses to ask. Now there's no friendly face to keep an eye on the baby while she nips to the toilet. No midwife rushing over to answer the bell if Nicola needs some help. No comforting eyes if she makes a mistake.

And there's nowhere lonelier in the dead of night than your bedroom with a baby screaming blue murder and your mum sighing through the paper-thin walls.

She tries her with a bottle again. Even though she only had one an hour earlier. Eliza spits the teat out. Her tongue is strong and outraged. It makes her cry even more.

Nicola's crying too. She catches sight of her reflection in the darkened window in the crack between the curtains and sees great wet streak marks all the way down her cheeks. She looks outside into the darkness. Sees the drop below. Imagines, in a daze, opening the window and letting Eliza fall. How her blanket would billow to the floor like a parachute after the tiny body.

The image is shocking. Frightening. It makes her gasp in horror.

She's doing really badly. She knew all along that she

couldn't cope.

By half past midnight Nicola feels like a corpse in a trance. She's become so used to Eliza screaming that she can't hear anything else. She's made tracks in the carpet from pacing. She needs help but she doesn't know who to ask. There is, in the early hours of a cold March morning, nobody.

The collar around Eliza's babygrow is wet from one of their tears. Her knees are drawn high. Her voice is squeaky from so much screaming. She is starting to sound like an animal in pain. Her skin is hot and damp from her distress.

Nicola is standing at the window wondering desperately if she should call a doctor. Eliza's knees bump against Nicola's ribs as her mum pushes open the door. This is what Nicola has been dreading. She steels herself for the barrage of criticism which is bound to follow. *'You can't cope.'*, *'Where did you ever get the idea that this would be easy?'*, *'You've made your bed – now you'll have to lie in it.'* etc. etc. . . .

Her mum looks old. She's wearing a nightshirt which is inside out and has a coffee stain on the front. She's barefoot and there are lilac veins which stick out at her ankles. Her hair is wild and messy and her mouth is as sour as vinegar.

'Sorry, Mum – I can't seem to stop her—'

But she's interrupted. Interrupted and shocked when, instead of standing in the doorway shouting abuse, Nicola's mum takes some steps forward. Forward, towards the baby. Her arms are outstretched and her fingers angle in to slide between Nicola and Eliza.

Her voice is amazingly kind. Tired, but kind all the same.

'Give her here,' she whispers. Nicola watches as her mum draws Eliza into her chest like she was used to it.

Immediately, there's a softening in the whole of her mother's body. Her spine seems to sag, her shoulders sink and her face somehow gains curves. Nicola can't believe what she's seeing. But she knows she shouldn't say anything. Nicola's mum, if nothing else, is a very proud woman and in all her seventeen years of life, Nicola has never known her to admit that she's wrong or go back on her word.

So, clamping her mouth tightly shut, Nicola watches wide-eyed as grandmother and granddaughter start to rock to and fro.

At last there's a slight rise to Nicola's mum's lips. Eliza, surprised at this new pair of arms, begins to quieten down.

'I think she's got colic.' Her mum whispers gently into the face of her granddaughter.

'What's that?'

Another gentle smile. 'It's like baby indigestion. You got it all the time when you were her age.' Her mum offers a smile.

'Really?' Her mum rarely talks about when Nicola was a baby. Nicola gets a feeling that this was a bad time for her mum. She thinks it might be because this was when her dad moved out.

Her mum nods. 'You'll need to get some colic drops from the chemist tomorrow. I think she's old enough to have them. But you'll have to check.' She rocks. She coos. She smiles. Nicola just stares.

As the screams turn to murmurs and Eliza's eyes begin to

droop, her mum looks up at Nicola by the window. 'You look worn out. I'll take her for a bit. Let you get some sleep.'

Too shocked to argue, or even to string a sentence together, Nicola nods. She watches as her mum cradles Eliza in one arm and picks up the Moses basket with the other.

'Just for an hour or so. I'll be fine after that . . .'

But her mum's already left the room and there's this layer of silence in her bedroom which feels like the softest feather quilt.

Not caring that she's still got her jeans on and they're digging into her waist; not bothering with a feather stalk in the pillow which juts into her temple; without taking off her make-up, applying spot cream or cleaning her teeth, Nicola flops on to her bed, where she gives in to everything.

And she sleeps.
And she sleeps.
And she sleeps.

Several days later, on a cold day, with a few flecks of snow left in the March air, two figures and a buggy move down the road.

To Nicola, it is like finding her old self again. Like discovering a missing jewel from a favourite bracelet; like losing your phone then finding it; like not sleeping in your bed for seven weeks and then being able to sink into it. The feeling of walking down the road with your oldest, most trusted friend is equal to nothing on earth. And Nicola's lungs feel like bursting with it. She can't stop smiling. She wouldn't know how to stop. Olivia seems just as happy, if a little quieter about it.

Nicola pushes the buggy. Eliza, more used to the outside air and the light now, is blinking happily. Nicola wishes the walk could last for ever.

'You sure he won't be there?' she asks nervously.

They are about to embark on step one of Olivia's mission. And although anxious, Nicola would follow Olivia through a pit full of snakes if it meant that she could have her friendship back.

Olivia nods. 'Yeah – Saturday afternoon he goes out running. Don't you remember?'

Nicola doesn't like to say that life before Eliza is pretty much forgotten mush.

Olivia glances at her friend. 'And the bag's got anything she'll need?'

'Think so. If she needs a bottle then there's one made up. But we're not going to be long anyway, are we?' Her voice wavers slightly.

Olivia shakes her head. 'Just enough time to get the message across.'

Nicola fixes her eyes on the top of Eliza's head and watches the vision blur. She wonders what it must feel like to be as strong as Olivia.

The sun slips briefly between some clouds: It throws their shadows across the road. They look long and rangy and assured. Like two grown-up women with a pushchair.

Jonty's bungalow is five minutes away. It's a small semi, in a cul-de-sac which backs on to a field dotted with cows. Like all of its neighbours, the bungalow sports three white plastic windows at the front and a chirpy looking pot by the door. They stand on the gravel path leading up to it. The wheels of the pushchair make a crunching sound then come to a halt, which Nicola isn't used to. It's easier to drag the buggy backwards.

At the door Olivia glances at Nicola. She raises her eyebrows. 'Ready?'

Nicola's shaking. The quiver in her forearms flutters down to her hands, which in turn are on the handles. She watches the way the buggy vibrates. But she inhales and nods.

Olivia, before reaching for the doorbell, presses her fingers on to Nicola's wrist. 'It'll be OK. He needs to take responsibility.'

Nicola feels the tender pressure on her arm and remains unconvinced. *Not sure about that.*

The doorbell is brash. Its electronic loudness inside the house widens Eliza's eyes. She looks especially cute today in a padded red coat designed to look like a ladybird. It was donated by a charity. Nicola's not sure which one.

A moving blue haze behind the frosted glass.

Nicola feels her mouth go dry. Jonty's nan is one of those small, wiry women who seem to have energy and strength beyond their age. She has orange lipstick smeared on her lips and her eyebrows are drawn on to her forehead with pencil. Her hair is yellow and fuzzy, cropped close to her head. She might be intimidating and pushy, but the smile on her face when she catches sight of Olivia through the glass immediately softens the atmosphere. She throws wide the door.

79

'Olivia, well how are you?'

Olivia smiles back. 'I'm fine, thank you.'

It sometimes feels like everybody likes Olivia.

Nicola watches the older woman scan iron-grey eyes over Olivia's features. Nothing. Nicola realizes, gets past this woman. After a couple of seconds she looks towards Nicola and Eliza. Her expression falls for a split second but brightens when she looks back at Olivia. 'To what do I owe this pleasure then? Jonty's out you know?'

Olivia nods.

'Yeah . . . I know . . . we thought he might be.' Her elbow bumps against Nicola's.

She's nervous.

'Are you feeling all right today?' Olivia continues. 'I mean, do you want to sit down or something? Because what I've got to say might come as a bit of a shock.'

Jonty's nan frowns. Glances from Olivia to Nicola then down to the baby. Then she looks away.

'I'm fine,' she mutters. But her fingers grip fiercely on to the latch of the front door. This woman might be made of stern stuff, but her knuckles are shell-white.

Several tense seconds where a blackbird explodes into song in the shadows of the terracotta pot. Nicola can't believe its bad timing.

Olivia takes a breath. She waves her hand at Eliza whose jewel eyes stare ahead at the elderly woman by the door. 'Um, Mrs Jones. I'd like you to meet Eliza.' All three pairs of adult eyes bathe the baby. Eliza squirms happily. 'She's Nicola's.

But . . . but . . . also she's Jonty's.'

Nicola watches the colour drain from the old lady's skin, the fingers grip tighter on the door. She's scared.

But Olivia goes on, the information streaming out of her.

'We were wondering if you might like to have her for an hour. To see how you get on. We'd only go down the road. Just to get a few bits. Nappies and stuff. We'd be back very soon. Only we thought you might like to meet her. With her being your great-granddaughter and everything . . .'

It feels cruel, on this bright, blustery March afternoon, to watch a very proud elderly woman struggle to find her words.

So cruel in fact that Nicola has to look at the ground instead.

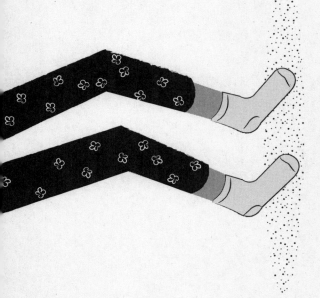

alice
april

Maybe Alice is a bad person. All her parents want is for her to have some friends. Maybe she is doing something wrong.

So, she spends her breaktime doing the same thing that she does every morning: a toilet stop. (This is normal. Everyone has to go to the toilet. Even popular people with blonde, perfect hair and pink lip gloss like Julia Smythe have to urinate.) And then she stays as long as she can inside the cubicle. Depending on who else is in the toilets, this can be as long as the full twenty minutes. These times are good. She can sit with the toilet lid down and inspect the walls for new graffiti or think about her animals and prepare for when she gets home.

But it is not always as easy as this. Sometimes – if, for example, Julia Smythe comes in with all her friends – people start to realize that someone is spending longer than the appropriate time in the cubicle. They might start to bang on the door or kick at it. Or even, as happens today, stand on the toilet next door and poke their heads over the side.

There is a shriek of laughter and one of Julia's lip-gloss friends shouts. 'It's weird Alice.'

'What's she doing?' Alice recognizes Julia Smythe's voice. She is probably looking at herself in the mirror. She does this a lot. Maybe because she is worried that she is developing teenage acne. This is common in year eight students.

Lip-gloss girl stares at Alice, and Alice finds herself going red. Olivia would be ashamed. She would know exactly how to react. She certainly wouldn't go red.

'Being weird, of course.'

Alice grabs the strap of her school bag and bites her lip,

85

thinking. She has to make a break for it. She has no way of being able to see through doors; the human eye has not evolved enough for this yet. So she doesn't know how many girls are out there. But she hazards a guess at four or five. This is the usual number of girls who walk around with Julia Smythe.

Her fingers are trembling as she tries to unlock the door. This is a symptom of fear. Lip-gloss girl laughs. 'Weird Alice,' she says.

Alice decides against eye contact. On this occasion, if she walks straight out, they might choose to ignore her.

The whole toilet now smells of the body spray which girls like Julia Smythe tend to wear.

Julia Smythe is the first person Alice sees when she eventually masters the lock and opens the cubicle door. She smiles. But it is not a smile of friendship. It could be described as a smirk. Julia is propped up on a sink and she is fiddling with some body spray. She squirts the spray at Alice but Alice does not need it. She used her own deodorant this morning just as Olivia showed her at the beginning of year seven. She told Alice that it was not a good thing to have a BO reputation at secondary, this was very important. BO stands for Body Odour as she found out when she googled it.

After the spray, Julia Smythe jiggles her leg up and down and laughs. 'Don't they have special schools for kids like you?'

Alice feels a hot sensation in her mouth. The best thing to do is just leave the room and find the second thing to do on a drizzly April breaktime.

She shuts the door behind her, but even in the corridor she hears the hoots of unkind laughter.

She keeps to the walls, knowing that this way she will stay out of the way of boys running about. Boys in particular can knock her down and not even notice.

People are not allowed inside the school at breaktime unless it is wet break. In which case there are allocated wet rooms. (The rain is not heavy enough today.) So everyone has to be outside, except when using the toilet.

Alice makes her way through the double doors into the drizzle. She wishes she could see her sister. Olivia might be in a kind mood and perhaps suggest that she stay with her until the bell goes. But Olivia is rarely in Alice's playground. She has her own sixth-form area and lots of her own friends. It would also be nice to see Olivia's friend Ben. He is a kind and patient person who listens. Her sister's friend Nicola is also a good person but unfortunately she is not at school at the moment because ten weeks ago she gave birth in the bathroom to an illegitimate baby.

The person she does not want to see is Jonty, Olivia's ex-boyfriend. He is not a nice person and commits domestic abuse. Although nobody else seems to realize this. At least she *thinks* he is Olivia's ex-boyfriend. He still comes around to the house every so often and pleads with Olivia to take him back. Two nights ago, when her mum and dad were at Tesco, as Alice was grooming her horse, Malachite, she could hear the sounds of male crying coming from behind Olivia's door.

Alice hopes and prays that her sister does not take him back.

Alice shelters against a large wall close to some other pupils who do not seem to have many friends. This is a good wall to stand by as there is an overhanging piece of roof which provides shelter and also some shade.

She looks around her and wonders how you make friends. It would be a very good thing to bring a friend home. But she has never done it. Her parents have told her that she is very clever and this can be off-putting to the people around her. Alice does not see why; it is probably just another one of those things which she will never properly make sense of. It is not like she goes up to people to tell them how to work out the thirteen times table without writing it down. You have to keep things like this to yourself. Olivia is always telling her. There are so many rules that she has to learn.

She checks the time on her waterproof watch, holding it into the drizzle just to give it a quick test. Five more minutes before she can go back to the safety of a classroom. At least there she can immerse herself in what she is learning and avoid comments about being a loser or a loner.

Lunchtimes are not quite as bad. There is Rocket Club on Mondays and Gifted and Talented Maths on Thursdays. The rest of the days she can eat her lunch and then go into the library where there is a lovely corner in which she can sit down and read a book. She is going through the alphabet at the moment: A-Z of authors. She is currently on C. But that is all right because she is only in year seven and there are at least six more years left at this school, should she make it through each day.

She spots a gang of year sevens who play in the netball team. She shrinks back against the wall. These netball girls hate her almost as much as the lip-gloss girls. She knows this. She was once forced to play as Goal Keeper by Mrs Heaney, the PE teacher, who was short of players. Alice's height caught the teacher's eye and she was made to stand under the goalpost with her arms at a sixty degree angle over her opponents' heads. She let in thirty-eight goals. A school record. She has never been forgiven by the rest of the netball team. Mrs Heaney has not asked her to play again. Yet Alice was extremely accomplished at working out a sixty degree angle without the use of a protractor. But nobody seemed to notice.

Alice presses herself against the wall. There does not seem to be an escape route. She swallows and waits. Kimberley White is the captain. She plays Centre and is very good at footwork. She stops a metre away from Alice.

'Hey Alice. What you doing?'

Alice hides her hands behind her because they are trembling. 'Um. Waiting.'

Kimberley takes a step nearer. 'For what, exactly? Your hundreds of friends?'

Alice shakes her head. 'The end of break, if you must know.'

There are titters of laughter from the rest of the netball girls. They stand behind Kimberley, giggling through fingers. Kimberley puts her left boot against Alice's right shin. Alice can feel it scrape on her sock. 'Nice shoes.'

Kimberley is being sarcastic. Alice is sure she does not really like her shoes. So she does not say anything. She hopes something might happen to distract the girls. A fire bell. An earthquake, even though they do not live on a tectonic fault plane. The bell for end of break.

Alice likes her shoes. She got them in the summer school when she did not know what the girls in secondary school wore. She is pleased with the purchase because the country is recovering from a double-dip recession and nice shoes are definitely a luxury item. They have bright buckles which shine when they have just been polished. Alice likes the shine but she thinks they might be too bright for Kimberley. Kimberley is wearing wedged boots even though the school rules state plainly that these are not allowed. She does not like how close Kimberley's face is to hers. She can smell prawn cocktail crisps.

'Where'd you get them?'

Alice gulps and wonders if this is perhaps one of those times where you can lie. She wants to sound fashionable. This seems to impress some people. 'Jimmy Choo.' She plucks the name from something Olivia once said.

There is a peal of laughter from the netball team. Two of them bend over in amusement. Alice does not understand why they are laughing.

'Is that a section in Primark?' Kimberley asks with prawn-cocktail breath.

Alice stares glumly. She is not sure what else to say. The laughter makes her hot. She looks over Kimberley's left shoulder hoping against hope for a friendly face.

There isn't one.

The netball girls crowd round Alice. They make her squirm. So many faces, so close up, make her feel scared. Her fingers press against the brickwork. She feels a nail bend back, then break.

She notices that the pupils beside her have left the wall.

One of the girls shoves her in the shoulder. It hurts a bit. She bites her tongue. She remembers how Olivia said it was important not to cry in these situations. So she forces back some tears.

'Ow,' she mumbles.

'Weird Alice,' one of the girls taunts. 'Where are your friends?'

Alice screws up her eyes so that she cannot see and then snaps them open. The light dazzles her for a second but then she spots someone she knows. Someone who is older and stronger than the whole of the year seven netball team. Over the heads of the five netball players she sees Jonty. He commits domestic violence but on this occasion she might need him.

'Ooow!' she cries again as Kimberley stamps on her left foot. She hopes that she is shouting loud enough so that Jonty can hear. He is walking quickly across the playground, his head bent very low. He looks deep in thought. But he looks up towards the shout. He spots Alice. She is sure.

Jonty is strong enough and old enough to scare the year seven netball team. All he needs to do is move towards them and they will scatter like frightened sparrows. But he does not. No, her sister's ex-boyfriend looks over with interest at the commotion. He narrows his eyes at Alice and falters for a second. If she was telepathic then she would be sending him the signals to be rescued. But she is not telepathic and she is almost sure that he isn't either.

And then Jonty turns away. More than this, he walks away. Away from the wall where the year seven netball girls are determined to make a living hell out of the last three minutes of Alice's breaktime.

She feels one of her shiny buckles get torn from her left shoe and sees its brightness get kicked over into the playground. It skitters, then lands in a murky puddle, where it stays for the rest of the day.

Alice is in the bathroom. It is half past nine and her mum has said that she should go to sleep, but she has too much to think about. The horses need their last groom before bedtime and besides, she has started to worry about school the next day.

She likes it in here. It is warm by the radiator and it smells of Olivia's deodorant. Also, if she puts her head against the wall there is a small hole where the pipework from the radiator feeds into the cavity and from here she can hear her sister. She has never told anyone this. She does not know if anyone else realizes it. But it is too important a piece of information to share.

Olivia is talking to her friend Ben. He came around about an hour earlier and they have been in the bedroom talking all this time. He has not been around for a while. Since the baby was born in the bathroom, a lot of things have changed.

Alice sits on the floor and rests her head against the wall.

She looks around her with the gentle tones of her sister in her ears and tries to relax. It is difficult to calm down, because this is the same room where Nicola gave birth to the illegitimate baby and it still feels strange. Her mum spent a long time cleaning up the blood and the other stuff and she knows for a fact that she threw away two perfectly good towels.

It is difficult to forget the images and sounds of Nicola moaning and screaming on the floor. But her sister's voice is comforting.

Ben's voice is lower than Olivia's but that is because of the male hormone testosterone. Boys' voices break during puberty. So Ben must have reached this.

'I don't even know how you can consider it,' he says.

She hears her sister sigh. She has been doing a lot of sighing since her best friend gave birth to the illegitimate baby. 'Because he pleads with me. Because he's desperate. Because he begs. Do you know he has cried every time he's come here since it happened?'

'Serves him right.' Ben does not sound very sympathetic.

'You don't know him like I do.'

'I know him well enough to know that he knocked up your best friend.'

Alice frowns. She doesn't understand what this means but wonders if Jonty has been committing more domestic violence to Nicola.

Olivia's voice sounds twisted. Alice imagines her sister's pretty face all screwed up. 'He tried to tell me it was a one-off, but I know it wasn't. Nicola told me.'

There's a bang and a laugh. One of those harsh, sarcastic laughs which does not mean something funny has just happened.

'When I realized it was his, I thought that he might have ... forced himself on her.'

'Attacked her, you mean?'

'Yeah.'

'Oh God. Really? You think he could?'

'Wouldn't put it past him. He's a bit handy with his fists, isn't he? But anyhow, Nicola told me how it happened.'

There's some sobbing. Then nothing.

Alice stares at the shower curtain, spots some mould which is growing along the hem. She should inform her parents that it needs cleaning, although she should not do this just now. Ben's voice interrupts the silence. 'You haven't forgiven her, have you?'

'No.' This word is shaky.

'So you've seen Jonty many nights since it happened, but you haven't forgiven your best friend?'

'Ben, she betrayed me. The worst thing you could do to a best friend. She had sex with my boyfriend. And I'm supposed to forgive her just like that? These things take time . . .'

Alice lifts her head in bewilderment. Her eyes widen in surprise. Jonty had sexual intercourse with Nicola. Now that is a strange turn of events. She tries to imagine Jonty with

94

Nicola but she just cannot picture it. Then again, she cannot actually visualize sexual intercourse at all. She has seen pictures in textbooks and none of the illustrations look like Nicola or Jonty. Does this mean Jonty is the father of the baby?

The next words from her sister are so quiet that Alice has to strain her ears and hold her breath to hear. 'Have you seen her a lot?'

'Yeah.' Ben lowers his voice. 'She was in hospital for ages. Livvy, she's really miserable. It cheered her up so much when you met up with her that time.'

'You're very close to her now, aren't you?'

'Yeah, we've been close for a while now, Livvy. Right now she needs every friend she can get. I think you should try to make up with her properly. For her sake.'

'Oh God.' Her sister starts to cry. Alice hopes that Ben, who is a nice person, will try to comfort her. Because right now, Alice cannot. She is, after all, supposed to be asleep.

Alice presses her thumbs together and notices how they go red around the nails as she listens to her sister sobbing. It is a horrible sound. She fiddles with her bracelet. The one Olivia brought back from a school trip to France. She remembers the week. How she was left alone with just her mum and dad to talk to. How there was no big sister to chat with. How she used to curl up every night in her sister's big bed. To breathe her sister's soft scents which were imprinted in her pillow. It was a hollow, lonely week.

It is too distressing to stay in the bathroom any longer. So she stands up, switches off the light, unlocks the bathroom

95

door and avoids looking at the floor where the illegitimate baby was born.

It's nice to think that Nicola allows her to feed the baby now.

Amethyst is going to need a good grooming before she can even think about going to sleep.

'Olivia, how do you make friends?'

They are walking to school, Alice in her school uniform, Olivia in skinny jeans and a hoodie. It is a good day. It is nice to walk to school with your sister. It does not happen very often. Olivia's timetable means that she often walks in later. It is pleasant to walk in the spring sunshine with Olivia, instead of being alone.

Olivia frowns and purses her lips. 'Um . . . it's a bit difficult to explain. It kind of happens without you realizing.'

Alice is doubtful. She cannot imagine having a friend without realizing. She has Sandy and she has her horses. But she is not sure if these count.

'But how do you get them in the first place?'

They walk out of the village, past the old farmhouse which gives Alice the spooks. It is old and run-down and nobody lives there any more. She has heard that it is haunted. She speeds up her steps.

Olivia moves her bag from one shoulder to the other. 'You kind of spot someone you think you might have something in common with and tell them something about yourself. And then you ask questions about them.'

Alice nods and tries to imagine doing this. 'But not about my farm.'

Olivia stops in her tracks. She gives her a careful look. 'No. Definitely not about that. That's the kind of thing you keep to yourself. Other people might think it's a bit weird.'

This is true. There are one or two people she has told about her farm and they have all laughed and moved away. She looks up at her sister admiringly. She thinks about the crowd of friends she has, how popular her sister is. The blood rushes to her head to think that she will ever have so many friends. She knows exactly why her sister is popular: she is kind and pretty and a really good listener. She is fun. She fits in. Alice will never fit in. Her heart is heavy with the thought.

Just one friend would do.

The school comes into sight. A sprawling campus of new and old buildings with crowds of people coming from all angles to meet at the school gates.

'So, if I told them my name and how old I am, this might work.'

Olivia sucks on her bottom lip. 'Sort of. Um, you need to decide that they're the right kind of person. And that you'd want them as your friend.'

Alice nods thoughtfully. It seems very complicated. Much more complicated than her French homework, for instance. She wishes there were a textbook which she could study. One that would take her through the process step by step. She could cross off each instruction like she does with Design Technology.

They meander through the gates with a throng of buzzing people. It makes Alice dizzy to think that she could make friends with any of these people. There are cries of greeting, hugs and high fives. Some of the people look sleepy and grumpy. Others like they have not seen their friends for ages. Olivia waves to five people. Alice counts. She herself waves to no one.

They stand at the entrance. Alice spots Ben over by the sixth-form centre. He has his head down and looks sad. She wishes he would lift his head because at least she could wave at him. Then she could be like everybody else. But he does not lift his head. She realizes that he has not been to the house for five days now. Not since the time that she sat on the bathroom floor and listened in on their conversation.

She nods over to him. 'There's Ben,' she says to her sister.

Olivia nods glumly and answers, 'I know.'

'Isn't he going to wait for you?' She is suddenly fearful of her sister's reply.

Olivia sounds vague, like she is not really thinking. 'Probably not.'

The bell for registration sounds; it hits a breeze and floats away.

'Aren't you friends any more?'

Olivia shrugs her shoulders like she does not care. But something about the set of her mouth makes Alice think that she really does. 'Um . . . I think he's a bit annoyed with me right now.'

Alice wants to ask questions at this. There are a tumble of

them on the end of her tongue. She opens her mouth and wonders how to broach any of them.

But Olivia seems in a rush. She hitches up her bag and takes a step away. 'That's the bell. I'll get slaughtered if I'm late one more time this week.' She looks quickly at her sister, nodding towards the emptying playground. 'And you need to go too. Don't you have assembly today?'

With her timetable firmly imprinted in her brain, Alice knows only too well when she has assembly. She had committed the timetable to memory from day two of year seven. She is good like that. And no, assembly is not until tomorrow.

Olivia rushes off with a backwards wave so that she does not see the one and only wave which Alice is able to offer on this April morning.

Alice has the opportunity to try out her instructions on that very day. She is in the library. It is lunchtime. She has eaten her sandwiches in the corner of the netball courts where hardly anyone goes. She checked on her dogs Agate and Onyx while she was there, but no one noticed.

She has her head in an Eoin Colfer book. It is really rather good and if it was not for the earlier conversation with Olivia then she might have been able to immerse herself in the story. She is in her favourite corner: out of the way of most of the activity, yet within eyesight of the friendly librarian who Alice really admires. Any trouble and she is within easy vision of a member of staff. And this is how Alice likes it. Always.

Dotted around the library are a few individuals sitting and

reading like Alice. It is a sunny April lunchtime so most of the school are outside enjoying the fresh air. There are a huddle of year seven boys over by the junior non-fiction, some year seven girls standing by the window and a gang of year eight boys ogling the graphic novels.

Every one of the individual readers is a prospective friend for Alice. She remembers how Olivia said they must have something in common, so all of these children with their heads in their books must have an enjoyment of reading as a shared interest.

Her heart glows with this thought. She could suddenly have so many friends.

She places her book down carefully, pushing a bookmark between pages 146 and 147. She is as quiet as a mouse.

She likes the look of a girl two tables down. She has messy blonde hair scraped back with a band and from where Alice is sitting she can see her knees jiggle up and down under the table. She does not look fashion-conscious. These people make Alice nervous because she does not understand changing fashion trends. This girl has on a school uniform and there do not appear to be any telltale accessories to suggest a strong liking for fashion.

With weak knees Alice stands up and walks towards the girl. She is reading a Jacqueline Wilson book – one which Alice read last year. It is a good book and she wonders if, later on when they are friends, they might discuss it.

In a strong, confident voice, because Olivia says it's not good to sound nervous, Alice blurts out, rather louder than she expected, 'Hello. I'm Alice Wilkes. I live at 28 Northgate Road, Prenton, Leicestershire, LE56 6TD. I am currently eleven years old although I'm due to be twelve soon. Who are you?'

The blonde girl looks up from her Jacqueline Wilson, startled, with wide, frightened eyes. She swallows and for a brief second looks around to check if Alice is speaking to her.

But the look is very short because it is interrupted loudly and rudely by the bunch of year seven girls who have moved behind the blonde girl. Alice failed to see them come over – she was so focused on her introduction.

Alice watches anxiously as the year sevens hoot with laughter. They literally cannot seem to contain themselves. They go bright red, they stuff fists into their mouths and they cross their legs in hysterics. One of them even mimics Alice. This, Alice thinks miserably, is especially cruel. She feels a flush rise up from the base of her spine. It prickles her neck and reaches her cheeks within seconds.

She knows she has done something wrong when the blonde girl snaps shut her book without even keeping the page. She stands up unsteadily while stuffing it into her bag, goes as red as Alice herself and mumbles something about having to go to a club.

This is an excuse. There are no clubs on a Wednesday lunchtime as all the teachers have to attend a meeting. She knows this for a fact.

She stands rooted to the spot in front of the mean, laughing year sevens, watching the blonde girl leave the room. They are making a lot of noise now. They are still laughing so much that some of them look fit to burst.

The librarian, who must have seen the whole incident from her desk, sidles up. She takes off her glasses and looks sternly at the year sevens. 'Girls – I am going to have to ask you to leave if you can't be quiet in here. Some people are trying to work.'

She places a hand on Alice's shoulder which is very hot. She speaks kindly. 'Alice dear, would you mind doing me a little favour?'

Alice nods half-heartedly, her brain still burning.

'Would you mind taking this book to the staffroom? Mrs Crawford needs it for fifth lesson.'

Alice nods again. Relieved to have an excuse to flee. In fact, maybe the librarian has done it on purpose. 'Of course,' she whispers, finding her voice suddenly broken and trembling.

She takes the book from the librarian and leaves the room. She might just have enough time after she has dropped off the book to go to the toilets and check on Quartz, Amethyst and Malachite.

Alice's favourite place in the whole wide world is the meadow at the end of her road. She likes it for a lot of reasons, but today it is because the sun is shining; it is a Saturday morning; she has no school and she is with her friend Sandy.

There are signs of spring. This makes her stomach feel light and airy. Maybe she'll be an environmentalist when she leaves school. She appreciates the environment much more than her peers.

There are bursts of birdsong, for instance. They chatter and jabber in the hawthorn hedge to her left and she pictures them tending to the beginnings of their nests and chirruping about their territory.

It is before nine o'clock. This is early for a Saturday morning. But she has never been one to sleep in. Olivia, for instance, lies in her room all hot and fusty till midday if she is allowed. But Alice cannot seem to do this. Besides, there is the farm to tend to and Sandy is usually nosing at her door from eight o'clock.

So her mum has agreed, now that she attends secondary school, that she can take Sandy out for an early-morning walk, just as long as she does not wake the rest of the house or return later than ten because of her piano lesson.

She sighs as she reaches the stile and inhales the scents of the moist meadow grass. The blades glisten with rain from last night. They look like frosted-up fingers, tilted up to the sunshine, wilting at the tips with silver sparkle. She cannot wait to walk through them. She knows that her jeans will be wet through within seconds. But she loves it all the same.

She thinks about her piano lessons. She enjoys them. She is an accomplished piano player and is shooting through the grades. Her teacher is a nice Polish lady with a funny-smelling house, who always claps her hands when Alice arrives at the front door as if she is surprised to see her, which is ridiculous because her mum has paid upfront, a term at a time, and consequently her Saturday-morning slots are booked well in advance.

They will do warm up exercises and then Alice will show her what she has been practising. Her teacher will either sigh in ecstasy or wag her finger if she has not done enough practice. Either way she will be happy by the end of the forty-five minutes. And as a treat, because Alice once requested it, she will play a piece for her. Alice loves these moments. Her teacher is excellent and the music – rather like the birds' singing in the hedges right now – hums through Alice's body, releasing something which is rarely set free in her stomach.

The only thing that she does not like about her piano teacher is the way that she closes her eyes when she plays. It always makes Alice feel slightly embarrassed to watch her and she is never sure where to look. At these moments she pretends to study the music in front of her.

She lets Sandy off the lead once she is over the stile. The dog bounds from one scent to the next, her tail wagging gloriously, her nose sniffing like she has found the dog equivalent of a chocolate fountain flowing over fudge. Alice lets Agate and Onyx off too and they dash into the wet grass in search of their horse friends who are over in the far corner.

It does not take Alice long to wade through the long grass to the corner. Her thighs become damp with rainwater, but it is all right because the weather is not as cold as it has been and also she has a spare pair of jeans draped over her chair in her bedroom.

She checks that she is alone, peering into every corner and looking by the hedge. When she is one hundred per cent sure, she shouts for Malachite, Amethyst and Quartz. She feels in

104

her pocket for the Polos which she buys every Saturday with her pocket money. She places three in the palm of her hand and holds them upturned and flat. Before long she is gratified to hear the thunder of enthusiastic hooves as her three horse friends come rumbling to her side. They stop hungrily at her palm and share the Polos between them, steam and snorts trumpeting through their nostrils. Alice cannot fail to feel a glow of happiness as she spots Agate and Onyx weave joyfully between the horses' legs.

From the corner of her eye she sees Sandy lift her nose for a moment at Alice's shout. But then the dog becomes distracted by something else and, head down, lumbers off in the opposite direction.

At these times, with the prospect of a piano lesson, with her six favourite friends by her side, in a meadow full of sunshine and birds, with no school for a full two days, Alice cannot fail to feel positively bursting with something like joy.

The piano lesson is alarming but good. Around three-quarters of the way through the lesson, her piano teacher is listening to Alice play. Her head tilts and her eyes are shut, but all of a sudden, out of the corner of her eye Alice spots Mrs Beilski put a finger to her cheek and brush something away. It takes Alice a while to realize that it is a tear. Alice has actually made her piano teacher cry. This is alarming and Alice is unsure what to do. She wonders if she is suffering with the same problem as Olivia. She has never had to console an adult before. So instead of doing anything, she just finishes her piece and stares straight ahead, giving time, she hopes, for her teacher to compose herself. There are a few seconds of absolute silence where she begins to feel the hot prickles of shame, when suddenly Mrs Beilski touches her arm and whispers, 'That was beautiful, Alice. Really moving.'

So these tears are not tears of unhappiness but instead of a strong emotion. She has experienced them herself on occasion. And she feels funny inside to think that she has done this to her teacher.

Sitting on her bed later on, having finished all of her tasks, Alice is suddenly listless. She is almost bored. She has done absolutely everything that she needed to do. She has cleaned out the stables and the kennels. She has groomed all three horses. The pigs and the dogs have been fed, watered and, in the case of the dogs, exercised. She has finished her title page for the Ancient Egypt project for Humanities. She has learnt the ten French words for various hobbies. She has written up her Science conclusion and she has even finished her Eoin Colfer novel. So now, with the prospect of nothing much else to do she decides to put her books away and go downstairs and see Olivia. Her mum and dad have gone to B&Q to buy a new toilet seat. She is not sure whether this has got anything to do with the fact that an illegitimate baby was born in the same room as the old one.

It is when she is packing her school books away that she notices something hard and heavy in the bottom of her bag that she was not expecting to see. For a few moments she does not know what it is. It feels alien and strange under her fingers between her Science folder and French book.

She has to check momentarily if she has the right bag. She does this by turning over the top. But there, sure enough, in her best writing, having used a laundry marker pen bought specifically for this task, are her initials: AW.

She finds herself scowling and reaching into the interior again. This time certain that she has the right bag. She grips the hard plastic tube-like thing and draws it out. It is green. It is plastic and it is a bottle. In a black Gothic-style font on the front of the bottle are the words 'Anti-Dandruff Shampoo.'

She scowls once again. She has no idea why the bottle is in her bag. Perhaps it is a mistake. Perhaps someone went shopping during lunchtime and put it in her bag in error. Key Stage Four and the sixth form are allowed out of school at break so perhaps this is what happened. There is, after all, a chemist in the village.

She is not sure what to do with the bottle. It feels heavy in her hand and not especially nice. Alice and Olivia use Alberto Balsam Sun Kissed Raspberry shampoo, which her mother buys every fortnight from Tesco. The fragrance is lovely and the colour reminds her of the gemstone kunzite.

But now she happens to glance up. She happens to spot herself in the mirror. And this is when she feels a hot slick of shame. Because she has a sudden memory of some girls in her tutor group in the rear corner of the classroom. In the memory they are giggling and laughing at something concealed underneath the table. She did not take much notice because these four girls are almost always giggling and laughing at something. Instead she turned her head and concentrated on the notices which her tutor was attempting to deliver. But then, towards the end of tutor time, Alice had to leave the room in order to deliver a message for the teacher. When she returned she was surprised to see that her bag was not where she had left it. Instead of being under her chair it was dumped untidily upon an empty table two rows down. At the time she did not think much of it. Perhaps, while she was gone, the teacher had wanted everyone to move their bags off the floor for some reason.

She remembers now how the girls were looking at her strangely and that Kimberley White in particular was almost bursting with laughter. Her mouth was pressed tightly together in an ugly line so as not to release the spurt of giggles which were ready to explode out.

So it is now, with a hot, itchy disgrace, that Alice peers at her shoulders in the bedroom mirror. There are light flecks of dusty dandruff.

She has never noticed this before.

Brushing at her shoulders she moves down the stairs to be near her sister. She has lots of questions to ask. But there is a noise from the lounge which stops her from pushing open the door. It is the voice of Jonty. She did not realize that he was here. She thought Olivia was alone.

'Why didn't you answer my texts? You've not even opened them. Look!'

There is a scuffle. Alice imagines her sister moving quickly. 'What were you even doing looking at my phone?' Jonty laughs in an ugly way. She recognizes the tone. 'You left it lying around. It's not my fault.'

Olivia's voice wavers like a little girl's. 'That wasn't an invitation for you to have a look.'

'It doesn't matter. When somebody takes the time to text, the least you can do is open it.'

Alice's head throbs.

Jonty's voice is low and hard and bitter. 'I can't believe you did such a thing. Leaving a baby like that. My nan was in a right state after you left.'

'We've been through this, time and time again. She needed to know.' This is quiet.

'Then it should have been me that told her, not you sticking your nose in like that.'

'I'm not going over this again. It's stupid. Why do you keep going on about it all the time?'

There is a tremendous scuffle then and Alice cannot quite work out what is happening. She can tell there is a lot of movement. Something crashes and something sounds like it is being pushed off the coffee table. Alice's heart rattles at the noise. She chews at her little fingernail.

'And I notice Nicola stuck her oar in. She's such a bitch.' These words are the loudest.

Olivia's next words are high and scared. 'So why did you sleep with her then?'

There is a silence then. And for some reason this scares Alice more than the movements. She stares intently at the telephone next to her. It is black and there is one message. Now would not be a good time to see who the message is from.

'Why then? Tell me why you slept with her.'

'Because she begged me. Because girls like her make it difficult not to.'

'And I'm supposed to just accept this? Just accept that she threw herself at my boyfriend and you couldn't stop yourself?'

There is another horrible crash and Olivia cries out.

'Jonty stop it. You're hurting me.'

Alice thinks hard. He must be committing more domestic violence.

She should go in because she cannot stand to hear any more of this. If there is one thing that she does not like, it is the sound of her sister being hurt. It's becoming a habit. Olivia needs to stop letting Jonty into the house and Alice needs to get braver. Maybe try to help. But her knees tremble with fear and suddenly Alice is sitting on the floor.

Olivia's weeping now. Alice can hear the tears and the sobbing. Her words slur with wetness. 'Go away, Jonty. You can't make me do anything any more. You can't hurt me. I won't let you.'

There's more movement. Horrible movement where something gets dragged. Then footsteps. And more footsteps.

'Get out. Just leave me alone.' The words are really high now. Alice has never heard her sister sound so distressed. She hears something get thrown against the door. It is hard and brittle, it might be Olivia's phone.

Then there are steps coming to the door; harsh angry steps

which make Alice swallow. Before she can think too much about this, the door is swung wide and the powerful figure of Jonty stands in the doorway. His fists are tight and there is a vein which is throbbing in his neck. Alice sees all this in a flash. What she does not see however is the door itself which bangs painfully into her knee.

'Ouch!' she shouts, shocked.

Jonty, who has been too intent on his own anger, looks down sharply to the floor and sees Alice. He frowns for a second as if he does not quite understand who she is. Then he glares at her and curls his lip as if she were a piece of spat-out chewing gum.

Alice has a terrible thought that he might be contemplating more domestic violence.

But in the fraction of a second that it takes for Alice to think this, he stamps past her, yanks at the front door and pushes his way out of the house.

Alice can smell the outside from where she's sitting on the hall floor.

The front door is slammed shut and there are several seconds of silence where both girls adjust to their solitude.

Alice coughs softly. She does not know why.

And then surprisingly, so that something catches in her throat, she feels her sister rush at her. She smells hot and moist and her hair is a mess. She flings herself into Alice's arms on the floor where she sobs loudly without restraint into Alice's neck.

Alice knows how to hug. She has hugged Sandy since she

was the sweetest puppy. So she puts her arms around her big sister and feels the judders and the sighs for a very long time.

Alice likes this – it hardly ever happens – but she feels upset for her sister.

She smoothes her fingers over Olivia's hair like it is Sandy's fur, which is lot coarser. But the effect is the same. It is soothing for them both. It's strange to feel her sister underneath her arms. Strange but really very nice.

It is funny how this is the second time today that somebody has cried in her presence. She wonders if she read her horoscope for the day whether this would be included.

Eventually the sobbing begins to subside. And her sister sniffs a bit and gradually pulls away.

She looks at Alice. She rubs her nose. 'Sorry about that.'

Alice shrugs. She's relieved when Olivia tries a weak smile. 'Bet I look a right mess.'

Alice assesses her and has to agree. 'Your skin is a bit blotchy. And your mascara has run.' She scans her face. 'Your red eyes and mouth don't look very nice and your hair is messy.'

She's surprised to see Olivia's mouth twitch into a small smile.

'Olivia,' she says, thinking of something suddenly. She moves her hand to her shoulders. 'Can you tell me what to do about dandruff?'

'Can you stay here with Eliza, while I nip into the shop and get some nappies?'

Alice feels nice. It's a big responsibility to look after a baby. 'Of course. I'll make sure that she's safe. I understand about babies now.'

Nicola nods and reaches for her purse. 'I won't be long.'

Alice grips on to the handles like a proper mum. She likes the important feeling in her tummy. She rocks the buggy like she's seen Nicola do. A rocking sensation is nice for a baby. She's read this in a book. She brings the books to Nicola so that they can share them.

Eliza stares at her. She's sucking on her dummy. One of the books said that the sucking reflex is a natural one, like she's sucking on a teat or a nipple and Eliza certainly looks happy underneath her blue checked blanket. Alice pulls the buggy towards a bench. This is where she will sit.

It's funny. But since seeing more of the baby, her farm hasn't needed so much tending.

She waits patiently, feeling the looks from passers-by. She wonders if they think the baby might belong to her. Maybe a younger sister or a cousin. It would be nice to have a baby in the family. Although she's not sure about all the smears and the mess and the crying.

It's nice that people are looking. Alice isn't used to people being interested in her. It's unusual being the kind of person getting all these looks. They're kind and happy and make a pleasant change from the horrible remarks which Alice normally hears. These people don't seem to care what shoes Alice is wearing or that her hair hasn't been washed.

One nice lady looks over the edge of the buggy, gives Alice

a wide smile and nods towards Eliza. 'She's lovely.'
There's a thrill in Alice's throat. 'Yes, she is.' More words
bubble out. 'But she's not mine.'

The lady steps back. She frowns a bit. 'No, of course not.'
'She belongs to my sister's friend. She's illegitimate,' Alice
goes on.

'I see,' says the lady. There are lines on her forehead now.
And then she walks off. Alice sits back against the dampness
of the bench. Eliza continues to stare, sucking on her dummy.

There's a girl with a strip of strawberry liquorice who's
standing by the door of the shop. She's counting something.
Her fingers flick open seven times. Then the counting stops,
and she comes over. She's looking at the baby.

Alice feels the sag of the bench when the girl sits down next
to her. She peers into the buggy. 'Nice baby.'

It is odd to have so many people talking to her. So many
strangers. There's another bubble of joy. 'I know. I'm looking
after her while her mum's buying nappies.'

The girl looks impressed. There's some straw in her fringe
and red on her fingers from the strawberry liquorice. 'I like
babies.'

'Me too. Only they take up a lot of time.' She grips tightly
on to the buggy handles. It's a big responsibility making sure
she's safe. But she likes the sound of her confident words and
she likes the approval in the girl's eyes. It's very unusual. So
she says some more.

'Her mum has to get up three times in the night to feed and
change and wind her. Every time she takes her bottle she has

to be winded you see – patted on the back. Otherwise she gets baby indigestion.'

She checks the girl is still listening. And she is. She's staring hard at Eliza and then at Alice. She has a pointed chin. Her liquorice is finished. The attention gives Alice more glow to her tummy. 'I've helped bath her many times now. I do it three times a week. Her neck has to be supported otherwise she can drown. Do you know a baby can drown in five centimetres of water?'

The girl's eyes widen. 'Really?'

'Yes, really. Because her neck muscles haven't developed enough to move if her face was in water. So she'd die a slow and horrible death breathing water instead of oxygen.'

The girl nods intelligently. It looks like she's understood. It's something that Alice didn't know before. 'Babies completely rely on their parents for survival.'

The girl nods again. Alice is sure that she's impressed. She's certain she's not laughing like Julia Smythe. 'Only this baby doesn't have two parents. She only has one. So I'm helping out to give her mum a break. I like to do it.'

More sage nodding. It really is nice. Alice searches quickly for more information. It's enjoyable under this girl's interest. The importance makes her wriggle. Her hands relax on the handles. 'I was there for the birth you see. Childbirth is long and painful, and I was outside the room and heard all of it.'

'Really?' The girl's eyes are now as wide as saucers. 'Did it hurt a lot then?'

Alice nods carefully. 'Yes. And there wasn't access to pain relief in our bathroom where she was born. Only a packet of ibuprofen which my sister uses for period pains, but I don't think Nicola took any.'

'No?'

Alice shakes her head. She feels her hair swing on her cheeks. 'No. So there was a lot of shouting and screaming.' The drama burns in her stomach. The girl looks extremely interested.

Alice is on a roll, so she thinks she should start describing the blood and the towels which were destroyed and maybe the other stuff which was left on the bathroom floor for several hours after. She takes a breath.

But then Nicola wanders out of the shop, a plastic carrier bag in her hand. She's smiling at Alice, peering gently at the girl. It's strange to be in the middle of a conversation, so that someone has to wait. It hasn't happened before. It's a nice feeling to have two people waiting for you to finish a sentence. It makes her blood rush about behind her eyes. She stops talking but the girl still looks interested. She has her head on one side and she's waiting. She's brushed the straw out of her hair.

She's a bit scruffy. And she's not a follower of fashion. Nicola takes hold of the buggy. Flexes her foot on the brake.

'Ready?'

Alice nods glancing quickly at the girl. There's a small smile. Alice smiles back. It's nice. Nice to talk to a stranger and have a smile at the end. It's the sort of thing that would happen to Olivia all the time.

The thought thrills her insides as she walks along the pavement with Nicola.

The meadow is picturesque today. Blurry, shimmering sunshine on damp grass. Frantic birdsong all around. Early-morning breezes breathe on her face. And there are bright white flashes as a trio of wood pigeons fly into the sky, making a clumsy racket as they are disturbed.

It could be a jungle. There is so much sound. If you listen too closely it can nearly deafen you. There is no room for any more noise.

Which is odd because it has been a quiet week. The quietest week in a while. Alice has settled into a calmer routine. She has found a new place to eat her lunch for a start. Down in the toilets by the caretaker's office. These are not used as much as the others upstairs because they are older and cold. They still have vast, thick pipes which are rusting and noisy. They smell musty. But Alice does not mind. She can eat her Cheddar cheese sandwiches undisturbed and this is a bonus. From here she is able to scuttle out unseen to either Rocket Club, Gifted and Talented Maths, or the library, which she notices the girl with the blonde hair no longer frequents. Alice has moved on to a Joseph Delaney book and she is enjoying it immensely. She feels safe under the protective eye of the librarian. She has not attempted to make friends with anybody else. She is apprehensive on this issue. So, for the moment, she has stopped the idea of making friends, even though she is letting down her family.

Her dandruff problem is being addressed. Her mum bought her some Head & Shoulders anti-dandruff shampoo from Boots after Olivia had a word with her. Alice quite likes the shampoo as it is the colour of beryllonite. The smell is good too. And after the first few washes the white flecks on her shoulders are fewer in number. It has not stopped the laughter from the girls in the corner of her tutor group however. But nothing except perhaps some sort of military tank will ever stop them. She has made the decision that her bag should be on her person at all times now though. So even when she has to go to the toilet or get something from another classroom, she takes her bag. She is learning fast. Just like she has with Eliza.

And even home feels quieter. Nobody seems to be visiting Olivia these days. Jonty has not called since the last domestic violence, and Ben and Nicola don't come. She misses these friends with their cheery greetings and their pleasant smiles and she knows for a fact that Olivia feels this too. Her sister has had several days off school over the past three months and she often looks very sad. Alice feels sorry for her sister but does not know how to make her happier. Even Sandy has tried.

Sandy is overjoyed to be let off her lead. She lollops off into the long meadow grass following a scent so that only her tail and hindquarters are showing. She bobs about and it makes Alice smile. She notices several shy clumps of daffodils dotted about here and there. There is a glow in her stomach when she thinks of these. They are signs that spring is definitely here. There will be bluebells soon enough too. They will be over in the bottom of the meadow underneath the shade of the trees. She looks forward to the blue fuzz of the future. She wonders about picking a couple of the daffodils to take home to her mum. But thinks better of it as she will only scowl and say that wild flowers should remain in the wilderness to keep the meadow pretty.

Her mum has been scowling a lot lately. It's something to do with the baby.

Caws in the trees above her from roosting crows make her lift up her head. She does not like the sound very much. They remind her of horror stories and there is something superstitious about these birds' dark shapes. But she pushes the thought from her mind. Superstitions are irrational beliefs which are usually founded on ignorance or fear.

Alice unties her coat which is knotted around her waist and settles it on the floor. From here she prepares to sit down and go through the process of tending to her farm. It is, after all, early enough for no one to be around.

She spends a happy twenty minutes chatting quietly to her animals. Sandy, every so often, makes an appearance, pushing her nose against Alice's leg to check that everything is all right. Alice threads her fingers through her straw-coloured fur to reassure her.

A pair of magpies appear close by; their machine-gun rattle and brave hopping distract her from her animals. She is surprised at the magpies daring. They do not seem to mind Alice being so near. They strut and pose at each other. She squints at them in the early-morning sunshine and sings, 'One for sorrow, two for joy, three for a girl, four for a boy!' which her dad had taught her. This is yet another superstition, but on this occasion it will not do any harm. It is not like there is anyone to witness her.

She then salutes them, shouting, 'Hello Mr Magpie,' and calls for Malachite who has used the opportunity to stray over to the other field. So it is with horror and alarm that there is then a loud rustle above her and a small hailstorm of twigs and last year's dried up leaves. She looks up, her eyes wide and frightened at the commotion.

In terror she sees a pair of legs. She feels the blood rush to her face as she remembers the last twenty minutes. How she was talking and playing and singing to real and imaginary animals. How ashamed her sister would be. Now she and Olivia are getting closer it feels all the more important to make her proud.

Now she has really let down her family.

The legs dangle in ill-fitting jeans right above her head. They reveal socks which are not a pair; a pink, spotted one and one which looks like it could belong to a man because it has the Guinness beer symbol on the ankle. Despite herself, Alice peers curiously. The ankles most definitely do not belong to a man. In fact, she would go so far as to suggest that these were the ankles of a girl, rather like herself.

'Oh God!' The words are said in a panicky voice from the person dangling in the tree. This person might be stuck. Or, worse, about to fall.

As a precaution Alice takes a step back. Her sister might

prefer her to flee the meadow in an attempt at avoiding embarrassment. But curiosity gets the better of her. She stays and peers at the pair of legs.

She does not have to wait long. With a shout of annoyance the pair of legs gives one last waggle and then something falls in an untidy heap on the grass in front of Alice.

Attached to the legs are a torso, arms, hands and head belonging to a girl not much older than Alice. The girl from the bench by the shop. The girl who was interested in Eliza. She grunts uncomfortably as she falls on to the ground. But apart from the breath pushed out of her for a second, she seems remarkably unscathed.

Alice is amazed and afraid. She has never seen anyone fall out of a tree before. In fact, apart from a few dog-walkers over the years she has never seen anyone else in this meadow. She feels slightly irritated. She has rather got used to the idea that this is her own private meadow, even though it is a public footpath and people have the right to walk, ride and cycle through it.

The girl in a heap in front of her looks a mess. It looks like she has not brushed her hair this morning because there is a fuzz ball at the back. And her stripy jumper is ill-fitting and baggy. Her trainers are scuffed and very muddy and she has a green anorak which is sliding off her shoulders.

The girl cheerfully grins up at Alice. Alice knows she has alarm stuck on her face like the strawberry jam from breakfast.

The girl stands up and then, to Alice's shock, sticks her hand out towards her. She realizes she is meant to shake it.

Like people do on formal occasions. A meadow is not a formal place, but Alice takes the hand and shakes it.

'Hello. I'm Bethany Rose Dennis. I am twelve years old. My birthday is 1st September and I like Harry Potter collectables. What about you? I remember you with the baby from outside the shop. I think you have imaginary friends. I can tell because I do too.'

Alice widens her eyes. The girl is smiling and nodding, waiting for Alice to reply. She does not look like she is laughing at Alice. She does not look sly or suspicious or intimidating. Despite witnessing Alice playing with her farm.

The magpies suddenly fly off. She feels a small glow. An ember of something hopeful in the pit of her stomach. And as they stare at each other for a few more surprised seconds, the glow slowly rises up her throat. Her mouth feels wide and warm and she can taste a bubble of laughter. It feels salty and nice. And then a few more, until she has to put her fingers over her lips because suddenly she cannot stop the giggles and the fizz of laughter.

The girl stares at her, a healthy pink to her cheeks. And then she does the same. She puts her hand to her mouth and starts laughing. They stare and laugh. They laugh some more and they look at each other. They bend over with laughter and take some breaths. Alice feels her throat expand to fit in more laughing.

If she looked this up in her favourite medical book it would say that this was a symptom of happiness. That is definitely a fact.

jonty
may

Jonty hisses out his breath and feels the tendons and muscles strain in his arms as he works out. Ten more of these and then fifty sit-ups. Then twenty minutes on his legs. He's pleased with how he looks.

He won't think of Olivia. But by thinking that, all he does is let images of her flood through.

Twenty press-ups as punishment.

Instead he thinks of his mum as he's in her old room. He's made it into his gym now.

She left on Mother's Day. One minute she was there, the next she was gone. He bought her a good card. Glitter on the word 'Mother', a nice verse. He was going to give it to her when he got back from his run. She liked a lie-in on a Sunday and he thought he might bring her a tea in bed.

Only when he got back, after a forty-minute run, she wasn't there. Her bedroom was empty. Her bed was smart and made-up, her pillows plumped high. Her wardrobe was bare apart from an old grey suit. It hung in the space like a ghost.

There was the telltale fragrance of her Chanel perfume freshly sprayed. He knew by its strength that it was only recently squirted. It was only a matter of minutes.

He now sees her only once, maybe twice a year. Depending on how busy she is.

And it is a worry; one which stays with him even now, several years on, that maybe she left because he didn't give her the Mother's Day card in time. Maybe this upset her. He should have done a shorter run.

The thought hangs at the back of his brain like her old suit left in the wardrobe.

So now, lifting weights, he remembers what the woman from anger management at school said and thinks about that card. It is still in its envelope although it's been opened and looked at many times. He keeps it in a shoebox at the back of his wardrobe alongside a few other things which he wants to keep.

Stuff to do with Olivia.

He's messed up big time. He knows he has. He's let the one person who meant anything to him trickle through his fingers. And instead, he's gained a snivelling, screaming thing as a result.

And now, God only knows why, but his nan has sided with Nicola and wants him to take some responsibility.

Thirty chin-ups on the bar, while he contemplates that. Sometimes he swears he can still smell his mum's perfume in the room.

And twenty press-ups to finish.

'Are you ready for tomorrow?' Jonty's nan plonks a plate in front of him. It's brimming with gravy; too full. There's a brown drip which dollops on to the table. He closes his eyes and tries not to think of the stain. Can't stand mess.

'Did you put butter in the mash?' He asks, staring at the pile of creamy-looking potatoes.

His nan sighs and shakes her head. 'No. You needn't worry, there's not a scrap of extra calorie in there apart from the potatoes themselves.'

She disapproves of his calorie-counting. She thinks it's

something only girls should worry about. He's told her enough times that it's because of his training. But she's still suspicious.

He tucks in and hopes that she's forgotten her original question.

But two pork chops later, while he's scooping up his peas, his nan tries again. Her fork is poised. The skin around her wrists is etched with sore-looking eczema. She's never ill. She might have wrinkles and look about a hundred, but the way she acts makes her seem younger.

'I said are you ready for tomorrow? You know . . . with Eliza?'

Jonty shrugs. 'What's wrong with your wrists?'

She pulls her sleeves down awkwardly. 'Nothing. I need some cream, that's all. Might be stress.'

He frowns. 'What are you stressed about?'

She sighs and reaches for his empty plate. 'As if you need ask.'

Jonty stares at the blob of gravy on the table. He knows what's coming.

'It's not every day you get told you have a surprise great-granddaughter and that your grandson doesn't want to know.'

He feels the familiar flick of anger at these words. They've been said over and over again for the past few weeks. He sighs. Gives in. Takes the four strides into the kitchen to retrieve the dishcloth. Swipes at the brown gravy on the table. Immediately he feels better.

'I've said I'll see her, haven't I?'

His nan, leaning against the table, the two plates still in her left hand, nods slowly. 'You have.'

'And I've agreed to talk to Nicola, haven't I?'

Another slow nod. 'Finally. After nearly three months . . . '

'So what's your problem?'

His nan moves her eyes from Jonty's face to the plates in her hand. There's the soft tick of the clock on the mantelpiece. Jonty rarely hears this. But today, in the silence, it enters his head.

'There isn't a problem, Jonty. I just want you to take this seriously. I don't think you have any idea of what you've got yourself into and I want to help.'

He sniffs. Closes his eyes and wants desperately to be somewhere else. With his mates he can lash out. Hit stuff. Snarl. Swear. But here, in this bungalow with his nan who goes lunatic if she hears anything close to a swear word, he has to watch himself. It pisses him off. But he's learnt to hold it together. Just.

His words come out a bit gruff. 'You'll be here, won't you?'

His nan smiles so that her eyes squeeze up. 'Of course.'

The clock seems to get louder.

Nicola and Eliza arrive at twenty past ten, Sunday morning. His nan is at the door before he can log off his laptop. He hears her chattering away. Like this is perfectly ordinary.

He stands in the bedroom doorway, looking into the hall, his shoulder embedded into the door frame, watching them

128

talk like they're firm friends. He doesn't know how women do this.

He catches Nicola's eye when she looks over his nan's shoulder. There's an awkwardness as strong as a knife between them, but also something else. Something Jonty hasn't seen before in Nicola. The thrust of her chin and the brightness of her eyes are new. This girl means business.

He lowers his head as she turns round and pulls in the buggy over the step.

Flashes of that mad couple of weeks flicker behind his eyes. He remembers how cross he'd been with Olivia. How everybody seemed to fancy her. How boys flirted and craved her company even though he was quite blatantly her boyfriend. How she didn't discourage it; some might say promoted it, with her wide smiles and loud laughter. How Nicola was there. Soft. Kind of vulnerable. Quieter. Like him, a bit pushed out. And how surprisingly thrilling it was. How she'd taken him by surprise with her interest and friendliness. Sexy. He shakes his shoulders. But ultimately stupid. That kind of stupidity ends in tears. And doesn't he know it now?

Because being yanked inside behind Nicola is the result of their stupidity: the baby.

He swallows. Why the hell did his nan agree to this?

Nicola turns the buggy round with a flourish, like a magician. He winces. Can't bear to look. His nan bends her arthritic knees and ooohs. Fusses and strokes at the baby. Nicola speaks to Jonty over his nan's head. 'Is this OK?'

Jonty shrugs. Wanting to scream, *No, it's not OK. Just GET*

129

OUT *and take the baby with you*. But his mother's presence hangs around the hallway and his nan has eyes as grey as gravestones. He knows what he has to say.

'I suppose.' He speaks gruffly.

Nicola seems anxious. 'I'm going for a swim.' She drops her eyes, 'I can't get much exercise with her around.'

Jonty knows. If there's one thing he's an expert on, it's exercise. He can see she's lost most of her baby weight, but even so, she probably wants to tone up. He nods again. Doesn't know where to look. Can't look at her body – doesn't want all that to start again – but can't quite manage to look at the baby either. So he stares at his nan's skinny shoulders.

Nicola fills the silence. 'I won't be long. Two hours at the most.' She gives him a weird look. One he's not quite sure about. 'And your nan'll be here all the time?'

He ducks his head. Ashamed. 'Yeah.' Hates that she has to ask.

Jonty's nan uses the buggy to support herself. She looks at Jonty, boring those gravestone eyes into his. 'We'll be fine, won't we?'

Jonty looks at the open door. Sees the space between the buggy and the outside and has a sudden vision of escaping through the gap. Running full pelt down the road, the wind whipping his hoodie, the freedom filling his lungs.

'There's a bottle in the bag and a change of nappy if she needs one. She'll probably wake up in half an hour. There's a fresh dummy in the side pocket and the wipes are in the front.' Nicola's prattling on but it's like she's using foreign words.

130

His nan's nodding encouragingly like she wants all this to happen.

When the conversation is over and Nicola's turning for the door, he realizes that this is for real; that he really is being left holding the baby.

Once the door is firmly closed he can breathe again.

His nan is grinning like a mad thing. She wheels the buggy into the lounge and stares inside with a goofing softness.

He allows himself a quick glance at the bundled-up figure. A pale-pink dummy and a nose the size of his fingernail. She's wrapped in a checked blue blanket and seems to be asleep.

He wonders what he's supposed to do. Stands awkwardly. His hands by his side, watching his nan coo and murmur over a sleeping thing which might as well be a doll. Women make fools of themselves where babies are concerned.

To his horror, she starts to unpeel the blanket.

'What you doing?' If it were up to him the baby could stay in exactly that position until Nicola returned. She seems safe enough, bundled tight in her blanket.

'It's hot in here. I thought I'd get her out.'

The baby sighs and her eyes flutter open for a moment, then the dummy slides from her mouth as his nan draws her from the buggy. He can't take his eyes off the expression on his nan's face; she has a faraway look. She stares at the baby and slowly shakes her head from side to side then glances up at Jonty as she lowers herself on to the sofa. 'She's got your eyes.'

Jonty's heart jolts. He even takes a step back into the

131

hallway. His calf bangs against the telephone table. He's never thought of that.

That this baby might look like him, be a part of him, has never, ever crossed his mind.

But what his nan says next has him even more jumpy.

Staring at the sleeping baby she whispers, 'Before Nicola comes back, I want a photo of you two together, for your mum.'

'What?' The telephone table clatters.

Unmoved, still entranced by the baby's face, his nan says, 'A photo. Your mum wants to see her.'

Gobsmacked. Dried-up mouth. 'She knows? You told her?' Jonty can't believe it. He doesn't want to think of her reaction. Has shunted the thought into the depths of his mind, to face up to on his mum's next visit. She comes maybe twice a year and stays for the day. It's usually the day before Christmas Eve and once in the summer. They're tense, crap days that leave him wired. Even before the morning is out, his mum and his nan will be arguing, and she'll have said something to make Jonty feel like he's disappointed her. She never mentions the Christmas card, the birthday card and the Mother's Day card that he will have unfailingly sent to her with his nan, the only person allowed her address. A stupid, insulting rule which pisses him off. But even Google can't seem to find her. He's tried enough times.

And he doesn't mention that she never sends him anything – except the obligatory twenty-pound note he gets on Christmas morning, unfolded from his nan's bony hand.

132

His nan drags her eyes from her great-granddaughter up to her grandson. 'Yes. I rang her last weekend.'

Jonty gulps – like they do in cartoons. There's a lump as hard and as bold as a conker in the centre of his throat. He wants to shout. Wants to ask, *What did she say? Will she ever speak to me again?* It's annoying how this still matters to him. Instead he stares at his nan. The words ram up against the conker.

The baby, in the crook of his nan's arm, shifts slightly. One of her hands flashes tiny mother-of-pearl fingers in her sleep. Jonty sneaks a look. Her features are miniature. There's a pink glow to her cheeks; she has small strands of dark, kinked hair which are sticking to her scalp. It hurts to look at her so Jonty looks at the carpet instead.

His nan starts to talk. 'She needed to know, Jonty. She's your mother. You know, when she had you she was on her own. She'll know exactly what it's like for Nicola. It was really hard, with no one else on the scene and me living far away. She wanted to keep her job and she wanted to keep you.'

So why doesn't she want me now? It still makes him angry, even after all this time.

There's a glow fizzing in Jonty's stomach. No one ever talks like this in his family. It's hard to stay still. He brushes his ankle against the table. He can't sit down.

He knows about his dad. He's been told about him once when he was five and once when he was twelve. After that it was made clear by his mum that she never wanted to talk about him again. So there's an ache in his stomach when he thinks that his nan might mention his dad. He holds his breath. Clutches the table with fingers like pliers.

His nan smoothes the baby's cheek with the back of her finger. She seems in a daze. 'I'm sure she'd like to think that you'll make a better dad than your father. You know – more hands-on, more involved.'

'That's not difficult.' He blurts. Hating the words which taste of spite.

His nan nods. She gets it.

His father's only involvement in Jonty's life is a fifty-pound note sent to him on his birthday. He always signs the card *Andy*. His father was his mother's boss. He was married. Perhaps still is. He doesn't know if he pays any maintenance because his mother refuses to speak about him. But he does know that he has his own children and doesn't want to get burdened with any others. His mother was frank about this. She said that Jonty was her choice and hers alone, and so she had to bring him up on her own.

Jonty hates the man. (Although he likes the fifty pounds.) He's never met him. But Jonty's seen the one photograph which he's allowed to see. His nan has a copy in an envelope with his birth certificate and passport: a smart-looking man with a suit, a short haircut and a tight smile hovering on his lips. Brittle blue eyes stare at the camera. He's sitting behind a desk with a phone to his ear. Jonty can't see or feel a connection with this man. Although on the rare occasion when he is mentioned, it's always this image which lingers behind Jonty's eyes.

'How was Mum?' This is a whisper. There's a crack between the question and the answer.

His nan screws up her face and looks out into the garden through the French windows. 'Oh, you know your mother. It'll take her some time to get used to the idea. She's still a bit shocked.' His nan squeezes a smile. 'And I don't think she's that keen on being a grandmother!'

He looks at his nan staring through the window and has a strange idea, one that usually gets pushed to the back of his head; the children, the ones belonging to his father, they'd be his half-sisters or brothers. He can't believe he's not properly thought about this before. Like this baby in front of him, they'd be related.

It wasn't just him any more.

A gentle silence passes over the room. It is broken only by the baby's soft breathing. Jonty sits on the sofa and watches his nan lift the baby towards the window when she starts to whimper awake. His nan points to things in the garden. The birdbath. The rockery. The gate. One of Jonty's tops hanging on the line. These are all things which Jonty's sure that the baby can't see, but she quietens anyway at the sing-song sound of his nan's words.

'It won't be long before she'll be smiling at you.'

Jonty frowns. His nan continues, 'You know, one of the best things in life is seeing a smile on a person's face and knowing that you put it there.'

And then his nan stands before Jonty. 'I have to go to the toilet. Will you take her? She is yours after all. You need to get

135

used to her.'

Jonty feels his eyebrows shoot high and he wants to melt into the cushions. But he can see how determined his nan seems to be, her eyes are aiming hard electricity his way. 'What do I do?' Sounds like a small child himself.

'Lean back against the cushions, hold your arms out and have your elbow ready to support her neck.'

It sounds complicated but he follows her directions all the same. He can feel blood rush behind his eyes. His nan lowers the baby into his arms. He feels the soft, warm presence of the infant's body. There's a milky, biscuit smell about her. It isn't bad. He stares. And when he hears his nan lock the bathroom door he finally speaks in a voice which is too loud to use for a baby, but he doesn't seem to have any control right now. 'Hello,' he says, 'I'm your dad.' And as her eyes spring wide at the sound of his voice, and their blueness bores into his, he has two fleeting thoughts.

One: Nicola's eyes are brown not blue. And two: the image of his own dad, in the photograph.

It's a murky day. There's a mist coming off the damp ground. The woods at the back of school are eerily silent apart from the call of crows which hover around the lower branches of the trees. Death-eaters. It would be a good day for a funeral.

A cluster of boys loiter in a circle. Their school trousers are low slung, and their sweatshirts hang off their shoulders. They're a pack. Hungry for something. Jonty stands on the outskirts, his hands heavy in his pockets.

On the floor is a kid in the year below. He's an emo, with studs and dyed-black hair splayed around his face. His hands and knees are in the mud. Jonty dislikes the kid. Emo-boy's crowd have been bad-mouthing Jonty and his gang for months now and he's finally getting what he deserves. Durant has this kid with his face in the mud. He's enjoying every last minute of it. There are beads of sweat above Durant's lip. It's ugly. The emo grunts as Durant's knee pushes further into his back. His sweatshirt rides up to reveal pale skin. Jonty spits on the ground. His hands delve deeper into his pockets.

The crows caw in dismay and rise to higher branches.

One of Jonty's crew rips open emo-boy's bag. There's a jeer as some papers fall and flutter from the open bag on to the grease of the ground. Durant picks up the bag and chucks it to Jonty. 'You want him, Jonty?' He sneers.

Jonty shrugs. He's unsure. There's something about the whole scene that he doesn't like. They all turn to him, even the emo.

'Jonty?'

He senses their unease. They're used to his direction. They can't seem to start anything major until they get his shout. And before today this would have come easily enough. But there's something Jonty doesn't like. And it's not the commotion in front of him. It's something inside. Something curdling at the bottom of his stomach.

Again he shrugs and looks at the kid in the mud. The kid returns his look. His eyes are a chemical mixture of fear and of

137

loathing. Their blueness reminds Jonty of someone.

Emo-boy grimaces under Durant's knee. Speaks with cracked words into the mud. 'You've … got a kid now.'

Like a whirlwind behind his eyes, the image of Eliza appears. And with this there comes a realization that his half-brothers or sisters might have blue eyes too. That this kid on the floor could even be his brother for all he knows. It makes him shudder.

There are boots at the ready. Fists twitching and flexed for action. The kid cringes in anticipation. Jonty knows they're all waiting for his response.

He holds the bag. It smells of stale apples and sandwich boxes. He fights back a gag. He takes a step forward, then two more, until his feet are centimetres away from the face of the boy in the mud. The tips of Jonty's trainers are as close to his mouth as you can get without touching. There's a four-second gap while no one says a word, and then Jonty drops the bag. It splatters in the mud so that the kid gets sprayed across his forehead and on his over-white cheeks.

'Nah,' says Jonty, 'leave him.' He turns around, offers his back to his shocked friends.

He can feel the disappointment stabbing at him between his shoulder blades. Someone shouts, 'You going soft, Jonty?'

He shrugs and makes his way back towards school. Perhaps he is. He's not sure. But as he leaves his jeering friends to walk through the mist, he has an unpleasant metallic taste in his mouth.

He spits on the ground. And thinks of Olivia.

Then of Eliza.

And then, strangely, of his unknown half-brothers and sisters. He doesn't even know their names.

Spits again.

The third Sunday of looking after Eliza, his nan suggests he goes out.

'No way!' he snaps.

'Why not?' his nan snaps back. Her hair vibrates with the shake of her head.

'What if she cries?'

'Then you bring her right back. I'm not suggesting you take her on a trek round the country. Only up the road. Stop being so pathetic. She needs a proper dad.'

'No, Nan. No way.'

His nan sighs. 'So this is it, is it? This is how we're going to spend the next eighteen years of her life? Cooped up in here, in hiding?'

Jonty swallows. 'I'm not ready, that's all.'

His nan flops on to the sofa and sighs. Her voice lowers a notch. 'What are you really worried about, Jonty?'

He thinks about the question. What *is* he worried about? His friends seeing? The knowing looks from all the nosy old crones in the village? Not being able to deal with her if she cries? People seeing he can't cope? The list is endless.

'I'm not. I'm not ready OK?' He hates the way he sounds aggressive.

She rocks Eliza. It's comforting to watch. 'People know. This village is alive with the gossip. I think it'd show all those people who are judging you. You could show them how you're taking your responsibilities seriously.' She looks him in the eye. The greyness is steely. 'That you're not like your dad.'

He looks away. That was low. She knows this is the one way she can get under his skin.

'Here, take her. I'm going to warm her bottle.'

Nan passes Eliza from her arms to his. They've become pretty good at this in the last couple of weeks. He'll even admit to liking the feel of this small sack of warm potatoes in his arms.

So, on the fourth Sunday, he agrees. Only to the shop. No further. Only to get his magazine.

It's the hardest thing he's ever done. Nothing compares to this. Not his first day at school. Not his first fight. Not even the day when he found his mum gone from the house. It's hard because it's public. And he knows there's no going back. People know now. He's seen the looks and heard the whispers. Word's got around like it does. That's what it's like in a village. But nobody's seen him with her; nobody's seen if he can handle her. The thought gnaws away at his guts.

His nan scuttles about, fussing over blankets and changing bags and sorting the buggy. Jonty stands at the door, holding his breath, his arms hanging loose by his sides, wishing he could go back in time.

Because he would. And he knows exactly what he'd change.

In the end he grabs the handles. 'Stop fussing,' he snaps, 'she'll be fine.'

He bumps the buggy out of the door before his nan can say anything else. Squints into the sunshine and sighs. Eliza, he's pleased to see, wiggles her legs in the brightness.

The walk up the road is weird; the most bizarre thing he's ever done. He uses one hand to push the buggy. The other remains in his tracksuit trousers. Casual.

It's a bright day. Bursting with sunshine. It glistens off the pavement where there's been an early-morning rain shower. Hedges explode with sparrows. An aeroplane high in the clouds takes people to other countries. He wishes he could be one of those people.

He sees neighbours in driveways, washing cars, cleaning paths, weeding borders. He nods at a few of them, avoids the eyes of others. If he didn't have the buggy in one hand then it would be a pretty uneventful walk up to the shop. As it is, it's like he's holding an elephant.

He negotiates the buggy easily enough into the newsagents. Makes his purchase quickly and exits the building as swiftly as he entered.

The mistake is getting complacent. He wonders what all the fuss is about. Doesn't know why Nicola moans so much. Thinks that a quick stop in the park might make his nan happy. That she'll be proud and won't think he's rushed the trip and escaped home at the first opportunity. Besides, a while in the sunshine with his magazine sounds good. Ten minutes, at the most.

He doesn't expect the park to be so busy on a Sunday morning. And stupidly, so that before he realizes, he's already pushed the buggy through the gate, so there's no turning back. People would notice the U-turn. He'd never hear the last of it.

Thankfully, most of the kids hanging out are younger than him. Primary kids he doesn't know. But there are a few older ones playing football down by the copse, and the unmistakable figures of two mates.

Brandon, the smarter and more confident of the two, throws a look his way. Jonty hopes they are far enough away to avoid seeing him wince. They saunter up the hill towards him and he holds his breath.

It's interesting. Eliza's presence seems to affect his mates. They're awkward. Unsure. Looking from the buggy to Jonty, to each other and then everywhere else other than back to the buggy.

Brandon nods, 'Jonty,' hardly pausing, he carries on walking.

Jonty nods back. 'Brandon.'

The whole interaction lasts less than five seconds. But it's five seconds where Jonty's lungs inflate like over-pumped tyres.

He's not stupid. He knows that this little incident will be up and down the school like wildfire. Can picture the new laughter.

Jonty Newman's weakness.

But then Eliza whimpers and he's dragged out of his

142

thoughts. He remembers what it was like to grow up without a dad. That raw, lonely feeling.

There's a bench by the swings. It's damp and saggy where one too many people have sat on it. And it's here where he decides to brazen it out. Ten minutes. He remembers the promise to himself.

He hasn't seen the girls coming up behind him. But he recognizes the voice as soon as he hears it and he can't stop the sudden swivel in his neck. The link with Olivia is too strong.

It's her mad sister, Alice. The crazy kid with some kind of syndrome. She always got on his nerves. She's the one person who he doesn't miss from that family. She's wearing welling-tons and a dress which is too short for her, but not in a slaggy way, more out of ignorance. And she has a friend. Someone even stranger looking, if that's possible.

She's wearing shorts which look like a skirt, the same type of wellingtons as Alice, and a stripy jumper. They look scruffy and dirty, like they've been outside for ages, even though it is still only mid-morning. But what is even more unusual is that they're laughing. They look happy. He's never seen Alice look so relaxed. She could be a different person if it weren't for the stupid clothes. They're talking rapidly, peering at each other, interested, like adults. It almost makes him laugh.

Oh my God, Alice has found a twin.

But they are each so absorbed in what the other has to say that they don't see the buggy. So the scruffy friend trips right into it. Eliza jolts and Jonty shouts, 'Oi!'

Alice ripples with giggles. 'Oh, Bethany!'

The girl looks up at Jonty, 'Oops, sorry.'

That's when Jonty sees Alice's eyes. They widen with fear when she recognizes him. He attempts a smile.

'Hello, Alice.'

But Alice is bouncing on her feet now. Her skinny arm reaches forward and she points at Eliza. 'Oh my goodness, Bethany. This is the baby again. This is the illegitimate baby. The one born in our bathroom. Next to the toilet. It's Eliza.' Jonty's breath swerves from him. But he nods. 'Yeah. This is Eliza.'

'Where's Nicola?' He doesn't like her wary look. Like he's taken Eliza without Nicola knowing.

'I'm looking after her, for Nicola.'

But then Alice seems to remember who is talking and fear gets the better of her. He can see it as it swells inside her. She yanks at her friend's arm. 'Come on,' she squeaks, 'let's go.'

Jonty frowns. He has questions to ask. Things to say. He stumbles to a standing position, desperate for them to stay. 'Wait a minute,' he blusters. 'How's Ol—'

But Alice is alive with alarm. She's trembling and pulls at her friend's arm like it's the most important thing in the world. 'Bethany, come *on*.'

She doesn't seem to have a volume control. Perhaps it's fear, he doesn't know. But he hears her words with goose pimples springing at his neck, as they echo across the park. 'He's the one. He's the one I was telling you about. You know, the one who commits domestic violence?'

The words are crystal clear, all the way to the footballers by the wood and the mums with their toddlers by the round-about. Everyone turns towards him. Shame roars up through his body. A forest fire of disgrace. The snap and the crackle of it under his bones almost hurts.

Eliza starts crying. He has to ignore the flush of blood in his cheeks and instead concentrate on his daughter. Something's the matter with her. She jerks her head from left to right and she squeezes tight her eyes. This is what he was dreading. Her little thighs pump at the blanket and she spits out her dummy. She lets out a high cry into the air. It's thin and reedy and has the mums at the roundabout look again with question-mark mouths. He can feel panic. It comes over his arms in a rush. He hates the way the mums are looking at each other. What would his nan do? He takes a breath and tries to think logically. What would his nan do?

He spots her dummy on the blanket and makes a grab for it. Stuffs it back in her mouth. But she jerks it out with her tongue, screwing up her face with distaste. He notices his arms are trembling. *God.* Eliza's wails get louder. Her face is an angry pink.

I'm not cut out for this. I'm not cut out for this.

Then all of a sudden there's Olivia's friend Ben. Ridiculous, with hair flicking around in his idiot face and shoes with a huge wedge. What a knob. The day couldn't get any worse, and if there was any way that he could disappear from this park in a puff of smoke, then he'd do almost anything.

Ben's head is up and his ears tuned into Eliza's wails. They're loud enough now for most of the village to hear. Mortified, he watches as Ben takes steps towards him.

Jonty stops still, his hands on the handles, tense. They look at each other over Eliza's howls. He's like a trapped animal.

But there doesn't seem to be anything in Ben's eyes apart from mild concern. He stoops down and looks at the baby, then back up to Jonty.

Jonty stands still, ready to leave at the first hint of a taunt.

Ben raises his voice over Eliza's shrill tones. 'She did this last time me and Nic brought her here.' He tentatively places his hand next to Jonty's on the handle, 'Can I just . . .?' He puts pressure on the bar so that Jonty has to remove his fingers. He lets them hang loose.

He watches as Ben shifts the buggy by about forty-five degrees, using his knee and the flex of his wrists.

Almost immediately, like magic, Eliza stops crying. It is as if Ben has found the off button. Jonty's mouth hangs open and his breath is forced into a sigh. 'How'd you do that?' Eliza is now perfectly relaxed.

Ben grins and shrugs. 'The sun was in her eyes. I've moved her so that she's in the shade.'

For the second time that day Jonty feels a flush creep to his cheeks. A fool.

Ben, though, is generous. He grins. 'Don't worry. I didn't realize either. Nicola was off buying ice cream and I was left with this screaming baby with the sun blinding her and I didn't even realize.' He shakes his head. 'Must be something to do with being female. Mums just seem to know. Maybe it's the maternal thing?'

Jonty snorts. 'Not all females. There was nothing maternal

146

about *my mum*.'

Ben cocks his head to one side. Eyebrows high. Jonty feels a surge of surprise. He's never said this to anyone before. But the words get the better of him. 'All she was interested in was her job. I always had childminders and babysitters looking after me.'

The air is soft between them. Ben's mouth twists. 'She left, didn't she?'

Jonty nods. Flexes his feet. Sees smears of grime on the toes of his trainers. Knows he'll have to clean them when he gets home. 'Best, really. She was crap as a mum anyhow. You know she never once went to a parents' evening? Never saw a show. None of the kids at school even knew what she looked like. I had to carry a photo around in my book bag at primary school – just to prove I had one.' His voice is a hot, embarrassed spurt. He looks away, into the sun, uncomfortable. How weak he sounds.

But Ben just nods. 'Must've been crap.'

Jonty sniffs. Shrugs. He can't quite believe he is having this conversation. He blinks several times. Shuffles. 'Not the best. Um, thanks for helping with Eliza anyhow,' he mumbles.

Ben grins again. He looks happy. Something's different about him. 'S'OK.' He starts to take steps to go. It looks like he's taking a short cut through the park to get to the new estate. But then he suddenly stops and turns his head. 'It's good what you're doing, by the way.' He nods at Eliza. 'Looking after her. Giving Nicola a break. I know she appreciates it.' Jonty swallows. He has to ask. It's burning inside him, hurting his throat.

'How's Olivia?' he asks.

He's seen her around school, of course, since the last time in her lounge. Even bumped into her on a couple of occasions. But she's never on her own. He's felt a squeeze in his chest. He's wanted to scream, *I still love you*, over the heads of her friends. But of course he hasn't.

That love. That love which started at eleven years old and is still there now, has a lot to answer for. That love, which was so muscular from the very start, had twisted into something horrible and skewed when he noticed how other boys looked at her. That love messed things up for him. And now he's got this massive hole where, by rights, his girlfriend still should be.

He knows there are new boys on the scene. Blake Johnson is sniffing around. He's seen the way she looks at him. He's seen how Blake returns the looks. And he knows there are parties. Parties to which he's not invited any more. Now word's got round, his popularity's shifted. How he's not quite top dog any more. How people have sided with Olivia. He's seen the photos on Facebook and Instagram and he heard them all talking the week following the party.

But it doesn't stop him wondering, or caring for that matter. He can't switch off his feelings like that after six years. He'd like to think that she still cares for him. He never goes to sleep without thinking about her. And he'd do anything to have her back.

But he also knows that this is unlikely now, and that the

best he can do is hope that she's all right.

Ben clears his throat, cocks his head to one side. 'She's OK, I guess. More or less back to normal. You know Olivia.'

Jonty nods. Pictures her lips, 'I—' he falters, not quite sure what he's going to say.

But Ben interrupts, crossing his knees and placing all his weight on his skinny left thigh. He plants his hands in his back pockets. Lifts his chin with curiosity. 'Haven't you spoken to her since you officially broke up?'

Jonty stares at the grass between them. Feels like shit. Shakes his head.

Ben's words are soft. 'Well, you should.' He waves a hand. 'There's loads you need to say to each other.'

Jonty slowly nods. Senses that the conversation is almost over. 'Yeah. Um, thanks.'

Ben turns round again, jerks his head over his shoulder. 'Talk to her.'

Jonty watches Ben as he picks his way through the bright green foliage which seems to have sprung up with the rain. He almost smiles as Ben lifts his feet in those ridiculous shoes to avoid the puddles. Jonty shakes his head.

He gets his first Saturday job in the garage up the road to earn a bit of cash for Eliza. The following week, he feels the buzz of his phone in the pocket of his jeans. He's had a crap day at school. One of his mates got suspended for slapping a kid from the school in town. He's pissed off and jittery because it could have been him. Perhaps *should* have been him. At the end of school Durant stood bad-mouthing him in front of the others. Letting him know that he had let them down. That he was inside doing a poncey revision class while he should have been with his mates kicking shit out of the enemy.

He thumbs in the passcode to his phone and sighs. It's Durant. There's a meeting. A fire and some cans on the hill. It's important he goes. Needs to show his face. Needs to improve his profile. He thumbs in a reply and roots round for his trainers. Bellows from his room through to the lounge where his nan's watching *Emmerdale*. 'I'm off out, Nan.'

'Where are you going? You haven't had any tea. I was going to do that fish.'

He rolls his eyes. His nan's obsessed with feeding him up. 'I ate a baguette when I got in. I'll take a protein shake.'

'That's not enough to feed a sparrow.' She bustles into his room, squeezing her hands. Her rings clink together. 'Where are you going anyhow?'

'Out.'

'Who with?'

'What is this, flippin' *Crimewatch*? Since when has this house been a police station?'

'It's not a house, it's a bungalow.'

Jonty breathes through his nose, shaking his head. Sometimes his nan's as barmy as a fruitcake. He's not going to tell her he's seeing Durant. He's not going to say about the fire. She's got a bee in her bonnet about his mates. Reckons they're bad news.

She pulls her mouth down so the creases in her face get

deeper. 'I thought you were going to do some schoolwork tonight?'

He pats his pockets. Has his phone and some cash from his wages. His trainers could do with a wipe down but it would mean prolonging this interrogation. Wonders about side-stepping his nan and making a dash for it, when the doorbell goes.

They look at each other.

'Who's that?'

'Well I don't know, do I?'

His nan shuffles out at full pace for her slippers. He hears the door, then a female voice. Recognizes the tones: Nicola.

He watches over his nan's shoulder. Nicola looks tense. All dressed up in smart stuff he's never seen before. She looks kind of good.

'Would you mind having her? Only there's no one home and they've called me in for an interview.' Her hands are tense on the buggy.

His nan's face, even though he can't see it, cracks into a smile. He can tell from her shoulders. 'Of course. Here,' she leans over for the buggy like it's a piece of gold. 'Let me take her.'

His bloody nan. She's a sucker for this baby. 'Nan—'

'We don't mind at all, do we Jonty?'

'I'm going out, remember?'

Clocks Nicola's eyes. They're narrow and desperate. 'I won't be long. An hour or so. Only it's River Island. I could do with the money. It's only one shift a week. But it's better

151

than nothing.'

He won't look at her. Thinks of Durant opening a can by the bonfire.

His nan's nearly peeing herself with excitement. 'Of course we'll have her.'

Eliza's squawking. Thrashing around under her blanket. She looks far from happy. Nicola looks down. 'Um, I think she's hungry. There's a bottle in her bag.'

'Don't worry. We'll sort her out. You go. You go and get that job, sweetheart.'

Sweetheart? Since when was this girl a sweetheart?

Nicola darts a look at Jonty, then back to his nan. 'If you're sure . . . Will you be here with Jonty?'

Why does she always ask that? It's annoying. Like he can't cope.

'Yes, go on. We'll be fine.'

And she's gone before Eliza can scream any more. Jonty rolls his eyes. Leans back against the hallway wall. The plaster's cool under his itching palms. 'What did you say that for? You know I'm going out.'

His nan's distracted. Sucking up Eliza in her arms. 'You can hang on for a bit, can't you? Just until she's had her bottle.' She's wrapping and unwrapping Eliza. Trying to calm her down. Eliza's wails are filling the hall. Thrashing about like an eel in his nan's small arms. He stresses that she might drop her.

'Nan, are you OK?'

'She's just hungry.'

He's not sure. Can't believe the racket coming from this small, dangerous creature. 'I was going out . . .' He sounds pathetic.

His nan walks through the lounge like she's holding a bomb. Eliza's crying's getting out of hand. He wants to shut out the noise. Hit mute. Hates the way the screams echo and bash against every surface. He has to follow her, even though all he really wants to do is run. Run like the wind. Run hell for leather.

'Get her bottle out the bag.' His nan's words are urgent. 'Quick.'

Finds himself fumbling in the changing bag. Hating Nicola. Hating himself. Hating his nan for saying yes.

Finds the bottle, cold in his fist. Hands it to his nan like it's a burning piece of coal.

She shakes her head. 'You'll need to warm it, Jonty. Come on, stop being stupid.'

Stupid. Stupid. Stupid.

Bangs it in the bottle-warmer and waits. Four minutes of stupid, stupid, stupid.

She won't stop crying. She won't stop fucking crying. Even when his nan sticks the teat in her red angry mouth. Her little face is screwed up like a demon in a horror film.

Horrible to watch. Horrible to listen to.

Eliza kicks and spits and thrashes like she's being tortured. All in his tiny nan's arms. It's too hard to watch. Too hard to listen to.

Sticks his hands over his ears. 'Stop her, Nan.'

'I can't.'

'Well, what does she want?'

'I don't know.'

This is horrible. His nan *always* knows. 'You must know.' His hands aren't blocking the screaming. The neighbours must think there's a murder going on. Can't believe there's *Emmerdale* all calm in the corner of the room.

Hates the shake in his nan's hands. Hates the screaming from this baby who can't be much more than half a metre long.

Can't take it any more. Needs to get away. Needs to hit something. Kick something to smithereens. Smash his way through the noise.

Feels the redness creep up his spine like a tide. Recognizes the signs.

'Oh God.'

But nobody hears because the baby's screaming is reaching a new height. Ripping at the wallpaper and in danger of cracking glass. It cuts at his insides.

The bottle gets shoved to one side. The hotness under the blanket spreads round the room. *I'm not cut out for this. No way.*

Paces with his hands over his ears. Has to get out. Can't let his nan see. Can't let her see how close he is to losing it. Thinks about the woman in anger management. The woman with the irritating voice, in the counselling room at school. What would she tell him to do?

Flies out the room, elbows bashing against the door frame

as his hands clamp his ears.

Flings himself into his bedroom. Kicks shut the door. Kicks over to his unmade bed. The pillows all crumpled where he was working. Wants to hide underneath it like he did when he was a kid. Hands still clamped over his ears. Feels tears. Stupid, pathetic tears. How has this happened? How the hell has this happened?

Bangs his head against the door. Once, twice, three times. Kicks at the door frame. Takes out a chunk of wood. Stupid, stupid, stupid. Slides down the door, a crumpled mess of patheticness. His forehead throbs.

But it feels a bit better.

Rocks to and fro. His hands now round his knees. Eliza. Nicola. Olivia. How has he got himself into this mess? If they could see him now, they'd be ashamed.

Sniffs back the tears. Angry.

Tilts his head. Then the noise. The noise, it's somehow quieter. Coming from the lounge. He sits for a few seconds longer. Feels his heart under his T-shirt. He tries to calm it down.

There's no noise now. Just the ticking of the boiler and some cars outside.

He stands up gingerly. Feels a wobble in his thighs. Smoothes his hands on his jeans. It's important to look calm. He tests his hand on the handle. He can do this. He can do this if he really wants to.

Wobbles in the hallway. Catches himself in the mirror. He rubs his eyes. They're red, a bit stunned, but himself all the same.

Takes a breath. Squares his shoulders, walks into the lounge.

And she's there. Over his nan's shoulders, blue eyes bright and shining, focusing then refocusing on him as he walks through the door. She's sagging over his nan's shoulders like it was there she wanted to be all the time. Happy as bleedin' Larry.

And she smiles. She properly smiles. So it hits him in the ribs like a kick from his worst enemy. She smiles. At him. There's nobody else. It has to be him.

His nan's all smiles too. Grinning when he reaches her eyesight. 'She had wind. That's all. Just a pain that needed winding.'

He stands in front of them. Arms by his side. Not sure what to do. 'So all you did was wind her?'

His nan beams. Nods. Beams again. 'Yes. That's all. Babies are simple, really.'

He closes his eyes.

'Do you want to feed her?'

'I have to go out.'

'Stay a while, Jonty. Just give her the bottle.'

So he does. Doesn't really have much choice. Has the picture of his nan shaking with the thrashing Eliza in her arms.

Sits down. Lets his nan settle the baby in his waiting arms. Lets Eliza tug and tug at the bottle, ferocious for a little thing. Looks down at her tiny mouth sucking for all it's worth. Finds a lift in his own mouth.

Ten minutes later, when the baby's lying happily in her buggy, kicking and cooing, he can at last pound the pavements in his trainers, it's the sight of her smile which rocks under his ribs.

He still hasn't managed to speak to Olivia even though he sees her almost every day in the sixth-form centre or around the corridors. She has her shield of friends around her. She seems to go nowhere alone even though her best friend Nicola now no longer goes to school. Her hair is cut shorter and she's taken to wearing an army jacket now it's warmer. It looks good on her.

And then something strange happens. Something which whips up his heart and makes him forget for a few brief minutes about Olivia.

He's been to school and come home early as one of his lessons has been cancelled. His nan hassles him about this. 'Are you sure?' She asks. Eyes as narrow as the hairgrips in her hair.

He sighs and opens the fridge for some skimmed chocolate milk. 'Yes, Nan. It's different in sixth form. If the teacher's not there, then you don't have to go. Stop getting so uptight.'

His nan wrings her hands. Pouts. 'Doesn't sound much like my idea of schooling.'

He withdraws his head from the fridge. 'Yeah, but didn't you have slates and chalk to write with? It's a bit different these days.'

She bristles and swipes the back of his legs with a tea towel. 'Jonty, you are so rude.' She smiles.

And he has to laugh.

While he is against the sink, his nan brings something into the kitchen from the lounge. It's an envelope and he can tell by her serious expression that it is something important.

'This came for you today.'

He takes the cream envelope from her bony hand. He turns it over and immediately recognizes the handwriting. In an almost reflex reaction, he checks the calendar hanging by the fridge.

The handwriting is looped and flowing in pale-blue ink. The same ink and handwriting that he sees every year. Just the once. On his birthday.

'It's from my dad,' he whispers. Heart belting around under his ribs.

His nan nods. 'Thought so.'

He looks up quickly, narrows his eyes. 'Does he know?'

His nan shrugs. 'I've not told him. But your mum may have done.'

Jonty breathes out. The kitchen is suddenly silent. Sun streams through the window on to the envelope.

He feels a prickling on his neck. Anticipates a written beating. Perhaps he's seen the last of the fifty-pound notes.

'What do you reckon? Am I about to be disinherited?' He doesn't add that he doubts that he was ever going to inherit anything anyway.

His nan stares anxiously at the envelope.

'C'mon, Jonty, open it, will you?'

Jonty tries to ignore the shake in his fingers as he scrabbles with the flap at the back.

158

There's a small piece of matching, cream coloured paper with the same looped writing and something behind, attached to the top right-hand corner with a paper clip. He feels the skin above his eyes crinkle up.

He reads in his head and then aloud slowly for his nan. It is only four sentences long:

Dear Jonty,

I have heard what you are doing with your daughter. It makes me very proud. So I have sent you something as a token of my admiration. Keep up the good work, son.

Andy

Jonty stops speaking quickly. He's afraid his voice might crack. His hands are now openly trembling. His nan butts in. 'What's he sent you? Come on, what's he attached?'

Jonty doesn't care. But his nan is frustrated, snatching at the paper. 'C'mon, what is it?'

So he turns over the paper and grins slowly, even laughs a bit.

'It's a membership card. To that new gym in town. You know the one with all the high-tech breathing equipment and the swimming pool?'

His nan claps her hands and jumps like a six-year-old. 'Oh, Jonty, that's brilliant.'

He laughs again.

But it's not really the card that he's laughing about. It's not the gym membership which is fizzing his blood. Instead, it's the final word of the fourth sentence. The three-lettered word which has never been mentioned before.

The acknowledgement he's spent seventeen years waiting for.

'Oh, Jonty.' His nan's grinning from ear to ear.

He stares at the letter, focuses on the word. Sees how the letter shakes in his hand. Ducks his head. 'Well, he took his time.'

Hears his nan sigh. 'Better late than never . . .'

Anyhow, whatever, he can't stop the small twitch of something nice in the corner of his mouth. The card is thoughtful. It was bought for someone who is into fitness. His dad has thought hard about this gift.

It feels good, even if it is late in coming.

It's a beautiful day. He's sitting under a tree and there's a light breeze. Eliza lies in her buggy watching the movement of the twigs and leaves above her. The grass beneath him is soft and springy. The meadow is deserted. But then again it always was.

This is their place. His and Olivia's. This is where they learnt about each other. From the age of eleven. He'd found it once when he was walking a neighbour's dog for a bit of cash. The cash he rarely got from his mum. A small glade in the dip of a copse. Protected from the wind, but a suntrap all the same. Two gnarled oak trees provide shelter.

It breathes with his memories: two awkward twelve-year-olds banging elbows as they gorged on family bags of Haribo; arm-wrestling; laughing.

Kissing later on. Older, wiser, more experienced. His hands

enjoying the familiar folds of her skin. The corners, the curves, the arcs. The scent of the perfume she uses. Still now, amongst strangers, that fragrance can make his ears ring.

His hands under her clothes. Her clever fingers doing the same. Fruit-flavoured breath. Flower-scented hair. Sugar from sweets left poised on her bottom lip. The flash of her pointed tongue as she flicks at the little crystals. His disappointment that she got there first.

Olivia with her hair whipping against her flushed cheeks on a freezing cold December morning. Her hood bundled as far down her face as possible. Him grabbing her hands, trying to warm them. Drawing warmth from hers.

She once covered him with leaves. Buried him. He remembers the musty, earth smell as they lay like feathers on his face. He liked the way they stirred when he breathed. But then there came a flash of how it must feel to be buried in a grave, and he sat bolt upright, leaves springing off his body. He remembers the softness of her mouth that day. He can't remember the last time they were here. This rattles him. Hopes and prays it wasn't one of those days when he might have hurt her. Won't think about that.

She's going to come. At least, she says she will. Brave from his dad's message and from Ben's few words of advice, he sent her a text two days ago. The first text since April. It took twenty-four hours for her to reply. Twenty-four hours in which, he guesses, she consulted with one of her many mates. Maybe even Nicola. He doesn't know if they're even speaking any more. Twenty-four hours where he thought he might melt, tormented. But a positive response in the end. And he takes heart from this.

He waits. And waits. The minutes pass as if they are hours. He plays with Eliza, lifting and jiggling the cloth clown which she has taken a liking to. Passing it over his face and making crazy noises. Birds jabber in the oak trees; the sun glitters through its branches.

Their agreed time of two o'clock shifts by. He starts to wonder if she might not arrive. The bright confidence of the morning begins to slide away. He gets scared. Wonders how long he should wait before giving up. Snatches a look at the time. Then another look and then, two minutes later, looks again.

Why the hell did he think she'd come? What could possibly be in it for her? He can no longer muster up the strength to distract Eliza. Feels relief as her eyelids begin to droop into sleep.

Five more minutes, he thinks. Then he should leave. Give up the idea as yet another plan which hasn't worked out.

And then he sees her. Climbing over the stile at the bottom of the meadow. Hair flying around her face in the breeze as she makes her way up the field. He sees that she's wearing her army jacket over a vest top and jeans. She has orange trainers which he's not seen before. It hurts when he realizes he wasn't there when she bought them – even though he didn't like shopping with her. That was because he never had any money. There was a time when she used to show him everything she'd bought. Now she can turn up in clothes he doesn't recognize.

Her face is pinched and there's tightness to her lips. Elbows are locked into her waist as she stands before him, a forced smile on her lips. She pulls her hair behind her ears. His own lips are dry. He scrambles to his feet.

'Hi,' he manages.

'Hello,' she says, and looks around her. 'God, I've not been here for ages.'

'Me neither.'

There are a few seconds of silence where the warble of some unknown bird lays down layer after layer of a song.

Olivia peers into the buggy. 'She's gorgeous.'

A small swell of pride. 'Yeah, she is.'

Olivia darts a look at him. 'Nicola says you're good with her.'

He shrugs. 'I'm trying.' *They're friends then.*

She screws up her eyes and he knows that she's thinking about her words. He recognizes the signs. 'No offence,' she falters, 'but it's a bit of a surprise.'

'You thought I'd ignore her?'

The breeze whips her hair over her face again and she spends time trying to tame it behind her ears. He itches to touch it for her, but knows he can't. His nerve endings scream, *I still love you.*

She sits down. Her hair immediately falls still. She picks at the knee of her jeans. He sits down next to her. Not too close. 'I wouldn't be the only one.'

It's a fair point.

She goes on. 'Can I ask a question?'

163

He nods. The smile fading off his lips. Nervous.

She opens her eyes wide. He could fall into them. He's probably spent the last six years swimming in them. 'What's made you so keen? How come you are now trying to be Dad of the Year?'

He smiles at her small joke. 'Oh, I dunno. I wasn't at first. I didn't want anything to do with her.' He tugs at some grass. 'But then I remembered what it was like as a kid . . .'

'What do you mean?'

'What it felt like . . . you know . . .' He nods. 'Without a dad and stuff . . .'

'Oh, and you didn't want that for her?' She nods at the buggy.

'No.'

'So you stepped up?'

'Yeah.' He rubs the grass between his fingers. 'I s'pose.' She nods.

A sigh ripples through Eliza's little body. It makes them both smile.

'Thanks for coming,' he says quietly.

Olivia links her fingers together. 'S'OK. After last time, I wasn't sure.'

He takes a deep breath, feels the blood fill the back of his neck. Thousands of words force themselves up his throat. 'Um . . . I wanted to say sorry, I guess.'

'For?' She's staring at her jeans.

He lifts his palms. 'For everything, really.' And then the words come. Like a torrent. Like an unblocked dam. Maybe

164

it's because he's sitting in this place – it's always done weird things to him. Besides, this conversation is long overdue. 'For bloody everything. For messing up. For sleeping with Nicola. For hurting you. And her. For being a twat. For losing you. For messing you up.' He's embarrassed to hear his words judder in his throat and he holds his breath for a few seconds to try to calm down. Lowers his volume a notch. 'I don't think I ever said sorry. Not properly. And I wanted to. Just wasn't sure how.'

Olivia is slim. The way she's sitting, for instance, her spine bent over, her shoulders hunched, picking away at her jeans, he knows that if he lifted her hair off the back of her neck, he'd find three small bumps of vertebrae poking beneath her skin. He knows exactly how they feel. His fingers hold the memory.

But he doesn't do it.

And then there's something ugly when he remembers pinching her there. Just under her hair at the back of her neck. She'd been flirting with Justin Caldwell and he had wanted to make her stop.

He looks away.

'Why did you do it?' Her voice is a whisper as she attacks her jeans with her fingertips.

He jams his fingers under his thighs. Knew this would come up.

'See Nicola?'

She nods. Just the once, like it hurts.

'Jealousy, I s'pose.' He checks her profile. 'There were boys after you. All the time. It pissed me off. You were flirty with

165

them. It felt like you were encouraging them. Sometimes I felt pushed out. And I think Nicola felt like that too.' This is diffi-cult. He's never been so honest. His words are short like barks.

'I wanted to show you what it felt like. Wanted to prove you weren't the only one who could have someone else if you wanted.' He sighs. 'It was shitty, I know.'

She's pulled her knees up to her chin now. He can barely hear her. 'But it didn't only happen the once, did it?'

'No.' He shakes his head. 'It happened a few times. We got a bit . . . obsessed. But then it was over. I think we were stupid. And the guilt was shit.'

'I told Ben I thought you'd attacked her.'

His heart hammers, a flush flares in his cheeks. 'Rape? You thought I'd raped her?' His eyes snap wide. 'Jesus, Livvy! I'd never do that! Surely you couldn't think I'd do that?' Stares at her. 'Look, I know I hurt you, I know I did some bad things . . . but rape? I'd never.'

Stupid flashes of shame zigzag behind his eyes.

She shakes her head quickly. 'Can you blame me? You were going through a pretty horrible phase.'

Embarrassment rocks him, blow after blow. I'd never—'

'It's OK.' Her words are still hard. 'She told me. I'd never—that you didn't. That she wanted it as much as you.' Now *her* voice wobbles. She sighs. 'It was the worst thing you could have done. Both of you. Can you imagine how lonely I felt when I found out?'

He nods, pressing a finger against his lips so that it hurts. 'Sorry.'

'Even Ben left me for a while.'

He couldn't imagine Ben without Olivia. 'I didn't know that.' Flicks his trackies. 'He's cool by the way – Ben. I was wrong about him. Are things OK with him now?'

She relaxes at his name. 'Yeah. We're mates again.' She shrugs. 'I think we are all OK now.'

No! No, I'm not. I still love you.

He watches as she fiddles with a stick. He knows her look. Realizes that she has more to say. He waits, expecting more grief. It's what he deserves.

She takes a breath. 'And why did you hurt me? Physically, I mean?'

He feels a flush creep up his neck, prickling under his skin.

'I don't get it, Jonty. I didn't deserve it. You weren't like that in the beginning.'

There's a dizziness behind his eyes. 'No. Think I panicked. Think I thought you were going to dump me.'

Olivia stares at him, pulling his eyes towards hers. 'But I don't get it. Why would hurting me keep us together? And where did it all come from? It's not like anyone was violent with you.'

Jonty winces. Knows the answer. He's discussed it with the woman from anger management. She forced him to look at himself. At everything. Forced up things which had been jammed to the back of his skull for years.

Remembers when he was four years old, how he was hit three times around the shoulders by his mum for not finishing his juice. How at five he was given nothing to eat for tea because there were still crumbs on the floor from lunchtime. How five slaps across his face reminded him not to do it again. His mother was a stickler for neatness and cleanliness and wasn't afraid of using her fists to push the point. She did this right until the day she left.

Jonty doesn't want to say it. Doesn't want to sound like he's using it as an excuse.

'I s'pose my mum pushed me around a bit. Maybe I got it from her.'

Olivia's eyes are steady now. 'You never said.'

'Well, it's not something you want to advertise.'

He feels her eyes on his skin, on his mouth, on the small hairs on his forearms. They lift under her gaze. 'Oh my God.' Her eyes widen. 'And that's when it all started . . . When she left . . . that's when you started hurting me.'

Jonty can't stand it – that she thinks of him like this. 'I'd never do it again. It's not the same any more. I've changed.'

'Why?'

'Having Eliza. It's sort of made me realize. How you shouldn't do that. How hurting people isn't cool. How it doesn't help anyone.' He frowns. 'I've had anger management.'

'Yeah?' She looks up.

'Yeah.' He drops his head. 'They talk you through it. Make you find ways of dealing with it.'

'And it's working?'

'Kind of. I still get angry and stuff but I know what to do when the red mist hits.'

'Like what?'

'Like counting. And thinking of other things and working out why you feel like you do. The woman – she's a bit creepy, but she says I should find out more about my half-brothers and sisters. Stop me feeling alone.'

'How do you feel about that?'

'Bit weird.'

She pushes her hair back. Looks at him through squeezed-up eyes. 'You wouldn't hurt the baby, would you?'

He shakes his head. Knew this was coming too. But gets it. Gets why she has to ask – why Nicola used to ask his nan if she was staying with Jonty when she left Eliza at their house. Tries to stay calm even though his blood is fizzing like a jet spray. 'No. No way. She's tiny and she's mine and she doesn't deserve it.' Bashes his knees with his palm. 'I'm here to protect her, not hurt her.'

She whispers, so he has to lip-read. 'You mean that, don't you?'

His head's heavy with it. 'I do. I'd let down my nan. I'd let down Nicola. I'd let down Eliza. I'd be worse than my own dad, as bad as my mum. She was a lot of things. She turned good things bad. If I took my anger out on Eliza then I'd be worse than them both put together.'

She lifts her shoulders. 'Even when you were doing bad things to me, Jonty, I don't ever think you really meant what you were doing.'

Stupid tears fill up behind his eyes. He squeezes his fingers together. 'I didn't. Shit, I loved you.' Grimaces. 'Still do. Think I always will.'

His words make a silence between them. A breeze hits the top of the trees. He holds his breath.

She sighs. 'And you'll always mean a lot to me. But—'

'It's OK. I know—' Brushes his legs. Can't bear it. 'Things are better now.'

'I can't forget it. I can't forgive you.'

'I'm not asking you to. I just . . . I just wanted to explain it.' Olivia drops her gaze. 'I've got something to tell you.'

He knows exactly what she's going to say. It's what he's been dreading.

He stares at the horizon and waits for Olivia's words like a funeral procession.

'I'm seeing someone else, Jonty.'

He closes his eyes at her use of his name. It's still velvet coming from her mouth, whatever she's saying.

He nods. 'I thought so.'

'He's nice. He's good for me.'

He winces again. She means that he doesn't hurt her. That he won't go sleeping with her best friend.

He coughs and tries to measure his voice. 'It's Blake Johnson, isn't it?'

He sees her nod out of the corner of his eye because he can't quite manage to look at her properly yet.

'Yeah.' Her voice is gentle.

'OK.'

It wasn't like he didn't expect this.

Taking a deep breath and feeling it wobble out as he exhales, he whispers, 'I've really messed up haven't I?'

A soft silence. Only the chirrup of a bird.

And then a gentle movement of Olivia's neck. Her hair sways from behind her ears like a curtain. She lifts her right hand from her jeans and gestures towards the buggy. 'Not entirely.' She nods at Eliza.

And then smiles.

Despite himself, he smiles.

With less of a wobble this time, feeling brave from her words, he lifts his head. 'Well you might think I'm heading for Dad of the Year, but I've remembered something.' She looks at him. 'I've only gone and left her bottle at home. Fairly soon she'll wake up. And when she does and she realizes that she's hungry, this whole field will hear about it.'

He starts to stand up.

Realizes he's babbling. But it doesn't matter.

'My nan says you should never cross a woman when she's hungry. And I'm learning that pretty fast with Eliza.' He places his hands on the buggy handles. 'I'm not that good when she cries. I kind of panic.'

Olivia giggles. A bit musical. 'Listen, Jonty. Do you want to come to a party?'

Sticks up his head. Temples thrumming. 'What party?'

She's standing up, her hands in the back pockets of her jeans. He remembers her thighs, how they can push against his. It hurts his stomach. 'Oh, nothing very big. Just the usual crowd. Just a picnic.' She nods at the buggy. 'Eliza's coming.'

He imagines them all. 'I don't think so.'

She shrugs. 'Suit yourself. It's just . . . just I thought it might

171

be nice for Eliza. You know, her mum and dad being there and stuff.'

'Will Blake be there?' Hates himself for that.

She's careful. 'Not if you don't want him to be.'

She's far nicer than he deserves.

Feels foolish. Knees wobbling like an idiot. 'Dunno. Um . . . can I think about it?'

'Course.'

Lets her straighten up and brush grass off her legs and arse. Lets her smooth her jeans around her ankles and walk off. Just like that. Doesn't say a thing. She just walks away in silence. He stands like a jerk. Squinting in the sunshine.

He spends the next five days as jumpy as a box of frogs. Snaps at his nan. Goes to sleep with a scowl on his face. Wakes up with the crease marks still ingrained in his skin.

His nan gets wind of it. Nicola must've told her. 'Are you going to this party or not?'

He's fiddling with his trainers, in the hallway, about to go on a run. It's the only thing which keeps him sane.

'No.' He snaps. Feels too big for the tiny stool he's sitting on which his nan uses to reach into the cupboards.

'Why not?' She's brandishing a duster like it's a flag.

'Cos I'm crap at parties. Cos it's not me.'

Her rings on her lumpy fingers glint under the light. 'Don't be silly. You never used to be like this.'

Counts to ten. 'I never used to be a dad. I never used to have to think about screaming babies. They'll all be watching me.

Watching how crap I am.'

She puts the duster down. Crouches by his side so he can smell the polish on her hands. Places bony fingers on his arm. 'Don't be ridiculous. You're a good dad. And you're getting better every day.'

Shakes his head. Nerves rattling for the escape outside. Needs the wind in his hair. Needs the pavements under his shoes. 'I'm going for a run.'

His nan looks up. 'Well don't be long. Tea's at six.'

It rains the morning of the picnic. He's never been so happy to see it splattering on his bedroom window. It'll have to be cancelled. Nobody picnics in the rain.

He's had texts over the weekend. One from Olivia, one from Nicola. Both giving him the time and the date of the picnic. It's in a park in the next village. There's a stream and some bracken and even a herd of deer. Not his type of place – a bit posh. He'd need his bike.

His nan knows. She's a wise old bird and there's not much he can hide from her. After breakfast, while pulling out the Hoover, she asks, 'When you were a boy, Jonty, can you remember going to places and seeing other children with their mums and dads?'

He sulks into the cushions, grabs at the remote, points it at the TV like it's Voldemort's wand. 'Yeah.'

'And you remember how you felt?'

Stabs away through the air, flicking from cookery program to sport. 'Yeah.'

173

She leans on the Hoover, her hip jutting out. 'Did you feel left out? Did you feel like you wanted a mum and a dad?'

Flings the remote into the cushion. Hates the way she can do this. 'Just a normal mum would've done.'

She fiddles with the plug. Her knees click when she bends down. 'No, she wasn't the best mum.'

Bitterness on his tongue. 'By a mile'

She sits by the plug socket. Delivers the killer question. He knew she would. 'So is that what you want for Eliza?'

Jabs the TV off. Stands up. Hates the friction which fizzes through the air.

Come two o'clock he finds himself in front of the mirror. Finds himself changing his T-shirt, spraying deodorant. Tells himself it's because he's been training. Cleans his teeth.

Finds his bike in the garage. Dusty and dry. Tests the tyres. Hard as rocks. Without thinking about it, without telling his nan, without even going back to his room to collect his phone, he lifts a leg behind him, over the cross bar and scoots out on to the road.

No going back now.

It has stopped raining. There's just some glistening under the hedges. The steam rises off the warming tar on the road. It takes him fifteen minutes. Fifteen minutes of hard cycling with a head as empty as he can make it.

He reaches the park before realizing. Clocks the car park. Rammed to the rafters with four-by-fours. Clattering children with scooters and bikes. Mums and dads hollering. Bags heaving with picnic gear. Seems that everyone's had the same idea. Maybe they'll cancel because it's too crowded.

Weaves his way quickly through the crowds. What the hell is he doing here?

Cuts through the swarms. Remembers where Olivia will be. He's been there before. Just him and her and an afternoon of sunshine and her body. Closes his eyes at the thought. Over the short pathway and through the gate. Cycles fast, weaving through the melee. Takes a short cut off-road. Knows where it leads.

Lets in thoughts. Admits he's nervous. Thinks he'll just show his face. Do the right thing, then get the hell out of there.

Two minutes through the flash of bracken.

Spots them before they spot him. Likes it this way. Still the chance to pull a U-turn and be back on his bed with his Xbox. It's like a scene from a film. Not him. Not him by a mile. It's a small patch of green, by the stream, under some trees. Only locals know about it. There's a couple of picnic blankets by the middle tree; some laughter; a barbecue smoking over by the stream; a Frisbee. This was his life with Olivia. She sets these things up at the drop of a hat. It has her touch written all over it.

Sees Alice and her new mate in the stream, water up to their knees, making a grab at a bucket. Alice is laughing. He still can't believe that bit. Doesn't remember her laughter.

Some speakers over by the barbecue send out tunes. Sees Ben fiddling with the buttons. His playlist no doubt. He looks relaxed; head down, hair falling over his eyes. A couple of kids chuck the Frisbee. Josh Strong and a girl from Maths. He's surprised to see Josh. Didn't know he was part of this crowd. Josh spots Jonty. Jonty steps back into the shadow of a tree. Doesn't want to be seen. Not yet. Hasn't made the decision yet.

Stands against the tree, scraping at the bark with his fingernails.

Hazy sun reflecting off the water makes him squint. Makes them all squint. Sees Nicola has shades on. Thinks she looks good. Better than she ever did. A baby seems to have suited her. Weird.

She's sitting on the blanket with Eliza by her side. She's gossiping away to Olivia. Her hands weave around in the air as she speaks. Remembers her fingers. Those girls can talk for England. Always have done. Doesn't know what it is, this connection they seem to have. Sniffs. They seem rock solid. Seem to have got through the fact that one of them screwed the other one over. Pretty impressive really.

Bites down on something jealous.

Takes a longer look at Eliza. Lets in a small bead of tenderness. It sits there under his ribs all strange and glowing. His daughter. Still feels odd to think these words. She's kicking her fat thighs, twisting a toy in her grip, making those noises he recognizes as happiness.

Inhales. Takes a step out of the shadows.

Ten minutes. Ten minutes tops, then he'll scarper. No harm done. Everybody's happy.

The wheels on his bike tick as he enters the scene for

everyone to see. Keeps his head down. Grips the handlebars. Reminds himself who he's doing this for.

'Jonty!'

It's Nicola. She's beaming all over her face. It's hard not to smile back. Anyone would.

'Hi.'

'You came.'

He nods. Keeps his eyes close to the ground.

'Hi Jonty.' Olivia's quieter. But he sees the look. Knows that she approves. Enjoys the thought.

Stands on the edge of the blanket. Awkward.

'Sit down.' Olivia pats the space next to her. He feels eyes in the middle of his shoulder blades. Hasn't seen Blake. Wonders if she's kept to her word.

'No Blake?' Can't stop himself.

She smiles. 'Don't think we're quite at this stage yet.' She gestures at the scene. 'Besides – I told you I wouldn't invite him if you didn't want me to.'

Puts his hand on his face, it's hotter than he'd like. 'I've got no right to ask though.'

She nods again. Thinking. 'No, you haven't. But I thought it was important that you came. And if it meant you did, then . . .' She lifts her palms. He could kiss her for that. She nods at the baby. 'Have you seen what she's wearing? She looks so cute.'

He turns to look. She's wearing a dress and frilly shorts. Her legs are translucent-white. Like they've never seen the sun. Thinks about sun cream. Turns to Nicola. 'Is she all right?

I mean, should she be in this sun?'

Nicola laughs. 'She's OK. I've brought a parasol with me. You can help me put it up in a bit, if you like?'

Likes the idea of doing something with his hands.

Nicola fiddles with Eliza's dress. 'Your nan bought her this.'

He doesn't remember stuff like that. But knows that Nicola does. Knows that she's as obsessed with fashion as he is with the gym. Has to smile. In fact, finds it easy to smile. She's cool, is Nicola. There's something soft but sexy about her. Remembers the smoothness of her skin and her lips when he kissed them.

He leans back on the blanket. Feels a muscle uncoil. Lets in some sun. Lets in some of the girls' conversation. Lets in Eliza's gurgling.

A pleasant five minutes pass without him realizing.

The sausage smell is good. Ben's over by the barbecue laughing with Josh Strong. Something – maybe a look they give each other, maybe the way Josh touches Ben's back – makes him think. An ooze of understanding. Smiles to himself.

Olivia's watching him. Shrewd. She can read his mind. She's got a small smile on her face waiting for his question. He doesn't give it to her. Doesn't need to. Just raises an eyebrow at her. She nods back. Puts a finger on her lips carefully.

It's good that they can still do this kind of communication. A relief that after everything, after over six years, there's still something. Leans back more. Feels another muscle uncoil.

Ploughing through two hot dogs, sitting between Nicola and Olivia, and it's another half-hour.

Watching the easy way Ben is with Nicola and the baby. Five minutes swallowing down jealousy.

Then he's rocking Eliza to sleep in her buggy. It takes fifteen easy minutes.

There's a game of rounders which he's quite good at. Some banter about school when Josh Strong brings over some cans. Arguments over music and selfies. A group photograph where he hopes he might be smiling. Sunbathing. Alice and her mate with a bucket full of river wildlife, sloshing it on the blanket in their excitement. The constant chatter over his head from Nicola and Olivia. A drowsy, warm feeling as more muscles unwind.

It's three hours later when he eventually thinks about going. Nicola's packing stuff up. She's on her knees rooting around under the buggy. Her jeans are tight on her arse. He needs to look away.

Jonty feels a hand on his sleeve. It's Olivia's fingers. He'd recognize them anywhere.

'Thanks for coming.'

'Thanks for asking.'

'I know it was hard. I know it's not really your thing.'

Sniffs. Watches Nicola stuff things in the bag. Her hair sways about in the breeze. It would be nice to feel its weight in his hand. Coughs. 'You can invite Blake next time, if you like. I'll be all right.'

Olivia squeezes her eyebrows together – like she always

used to. Her voice is soft. 'Listen, about your half-brothers and sisters – I'll help you find them if you like?'

There's a warm velvet feeling in his throat. 'Fancy yourself as Sherlock, don't you?'

'Might do.' Olivia's smile cracks her cheeks and her eyes are warm.

And for the moment, with a flash of clarity, he knows that this will have to do. That for today, and perhaps for a long, long time in the future, he'll have to make do with knowing he can still make her smile. Remembers what his nan said about seeing someone smile and knowing that you put it there.

There's some laughter by the barbecue.

The sun slips from behind a cloud.

Summer leaves rattle above them.

Makes a hasty decision. Thinks it's the right one. A soft shift inside him. It feels good.

He'll walk back home with Nicola and his daughter.

ben

june

Walking to work, Ben decides on something. It's nut-hard in the back of his throat. He has to accept it. There's nothing else for it: he's in love with Josh Strong. Can't help himself. It has him spiralling down into a vortex of agony. But it's there all the same. Love.

His steps are quick in the cool sunshine. Janey hates him being late on a Saturday morning. It's the one time when all hands are needed. It's the busiest shift of the week and he can't afford to waste time.

Five minutes later and he's there, breathless at the cafe door. Pushing it open, causing the bell to chime. And with the sound comes a hope. *Let Josh come in again this morning.* The shift starts predictably; Janey all ratty and tense after a hard night's drinking in town. Him and Seb – the other waiter who goes to a private school, but isn't actually that bad – sweeping floors and pulling down chairs to the cough and the splutter of the machines. The usual battle over background music. Him with his eighties indie, Janey with her modern day R & B. Janey, true to form, wins. It's her cafe after all.

The warm smell of baking permeates the room. Geoff, Janey's husband, is the best muffin-maker in town.

The first couple of hours pass as they almost always do, pretty quietly. Early-morning stragglers getting their first rush of caffeine. Bacon sandwiches and steaming mugs of tea. The usual homeless guy who slides into the corner where Janey sets him up with a free flask of tea and a sniff to say he has exactly five minutes to stay.

And then the more difficult rush as the cafe fills up,

although this is where he gets decent tips, if he plays things right.

And then, come late morning when Janey has finally wrestled with her hangover and cracked a couple of smiles, he'll be allowed a few songs using his iPod, when he's sure there's been enough business to make it worth Janey's while.

He bangs on a Stone Roses track and jiggles his way between tables. His friend Seb rolls his eyes and Janey just laughs.

'Too loud,' Geoff yells from the kitchen. But nobody takes notice.

Ben gets a chance to think about his evening during his break. He's looking forward to it. He sits with his feet on the coffee table in the tiny back room. A can of Coke in his left hand, a cheese toasty nestled on his lap. A night at Olivia's, just like old times. Him, Olivia and Nicola. *Final Destination 2* and a bottle of raspberry vodka. Perfection. Nicola's mum is having Eliza for the evening, something she does once a week. And this is how she's chosen to spend the opportunity. Ben feels good. He's pleased they're all friends again. It was difficult when they weren't speaking. Things are beginning to get back to normal.

He thinks about a cigarette. Reckons he might just have time if he's quick about it. He stands at the back door and inhales. Squints up at the sky with a watery globe of sunshine bobbing behind the chimney.

Let him come in. Let him come in.

He flicks the butt into the flowerpot which Geoff uses

when he thinks Janey's not looking. He's pleased to hear that his iPod's now bashing out some James to the baffled diners. It makes him smile. And his smile gets bigger when, after serving a particularly awkward customer who has to be persuaded that she ordered latte and not cappuccino, he hears the rumble of the football crowd.

He tries not to look. Instead, studies the order in his hand.

What if Josh isn't with them?

They're a noisy rabble who've taken to coming in for cans of Coke and chips after training. He likes them all. They're in his year at school. Cheerful and brash, they tease Ben about his waiting skills and clothes. They're not his group of friends. Too sporty, too packed full of testosterone. But he enjoys their humour and takes their teasing well. He knows that Seb's reluctance and annoyance gets him nowhere.

'Oi, waiter,' one of them yells, grabbing the Perspex menu and jabbing a finger. 'Five chips and five Cokes. Make it snappy.'

Ben waves his pen with a flourish. 'And will that be with or without something I've coughed up?'

Janey scowls from behind the till. But he knows she enjoys the joke just as much as his customers. He flicks a glance at where he's sure Josh will be. And he's greeted with the grin he was hoping for.

'We'll go without,' Josh laughs, sprawling across his chair. Ben nods, noticing how his legs are caked with dry mud. How his football socks are wrinkled with it, halfway down his calves.

Seb takes the order through to the kitchen and Ben is left at the fridge yanking out five cans of Coke. He feels a battering under his ribs. He stays longer than necessary with his back to the table; he doesn't want them to see how his hands are trembling.

Two kids with ice cream plastered on their cheeks take up his time.

The football crowd are loud and excited from their training. A table of young mums frown their annoyance. Janey raises her eyebrows at Ben. Ben just shrugs.

When the plates of chips are ready he and Seb serve the boys, plonking plate after plate in front of them. He watches how Josh devours the first few chips. He has a fascinating mouth. Full lips. Perfect teeth. He has to turn away and stand at the counter, breathing in, trying to tot up a bill.

'Ben?'

He spins round and looks into Josh's eyes. He watches as Josh slides a two-pound coin across the counter, his finger broad and stubby. His nail chewed down. There are three dots of dried up mud by the side of his eye. They make it hard for Ben to swallow.

Josh puts his hand through his hair and they both witness a haze of mud sprinkle on the counter around the coin.

'Can I have a chocolate muffin?' His voice is packed full of smiles.

Ben nods. 'That's one pound eighty.'

'You can keep the change.'

Ben slides back on his heels enjoying the attention.

'Big spender.'

Josh grins. There are crinkle marks by his eyes; they join the dots of mud together. He nods towards Ben's feet. 'Use it to buy some new shoes.'

Ben peers down at his creepers and lowers his voice. 'Fuck off!'

He can hear the exhalation of laughter as he turns towards the muffins.

'What's gay, Ben?' Bella dips an oven chip into her egg yolk and forks it into her greedy mouth. He watches as yellow spots the side of her mouth. He slides his own, empty plate to one side. He flicks a glance at his mum who scowls as she lifts the frying pan off the hob towards the washing-up bowl.

He sighs, feeling sparks jump under his ribs. 'Why?' he tries to sound casual.

Bella mashes peas against her final chip. 'Because Zac Jones said that that's what you are. He said it at school. In PE.'

His fingers fold into fists beneath the kitchen table. 'It doesn't matter, Bells. I'll tell you when you're six. But don't worry about it because it's not bad. It's just a description.'

His half-sister studies her peas. He knows she's not keen on them. But they both know their mum won't let her leave the table until she's finished. With a deep breath he thinks she thinks the moment passes. She's too intent on her peas to let it worry her. But it saddens him. He doesn't like to think of his sexuality affecting his sister.

Ben's mum and dad split up when he was young. She

remarried several years later and Bella became an almost immediate result. It took a while for him to get used to her. He remembers getting sidelined when Bella cried or whinged, and how this came as a shock. But as soon as she started walking and talking Ben was smitten. And now he thinks she's the cutest kid around – alongside Eliza, that is – and gets fiercely protective of her. Dave, his stepdad, is an idiot, but he seems to make his mum happy. And his mum is the best mum in the world, so this is all that matters. Dave has little time for Ben. Doesn't really get him.

'Finished,' Bella says proudly, popping the final fork of peas into her small button mouth. 'Can I get down, Mum?'

Their mum looks over to the table at Bella's empty plate.

'OK.'

Bella skips off out of the kitchen, her hair bouncing on her shoulders.

His mum sighs at the sink. 'You out tonight, Ben?'

He picks up the plates, stacking them one on top of the other, moves towards the dishwasher. 'Yeah. Olivia's.'

His mum nods over the washing-up. 'OK. Don't be too late, yeah? Haven't you got revision tomorrow?'

Ben opens the dishwasher and slots the plates into the rack. 'Yeah. English. I won't. Don't worry.' He likes English. Likes his teacher. It helps that Ben is good at the subject, usually achieving top grades with minimal effort. He's thinking of taking it at university.

Dave saunters in. He's wearing a replica football top and scratches at his belly. What a slob. How can his mum find this bloke attractive?

'I'm off then.' Ben pecks his mum on the cheek and inhales her scent of cooking and perfume. She nods.

Dave, in his socks which are falling off his feet, grimaces. 'You're going out like that?'

Ben stands still for a second thinking carefully of his skinny jeans, his creepers for which he paid a fortune and a top which he'd bought only last week from River Island. He looks good tonight and he doesn't need idiots like Dave to suggest otherwise. But he doesn't want another fight. So instead, taking a deep breath and feeling his shoulders stiffen, he sighs and tries not to sound too sarcastic.

'Are you offering me fashion tips, Dave?' He nods at the bulge of white flesh between the bottom of his football top and the waistband of his supermarket jeans.

Dave rubs his nose with the back of his hand, yawns loudly so that the fillings at the rear of his mouth can be seen, the skin on his cheeks turns a shade purpler, and then spits two words across the kitchen. 'Little poof.'

Ben walks past him. Determined to get out as quickly as possible, but even so, he can't avoid the whistle of disapproval coming from his mum at the sink.

Let them battle it out, he thinks. *Don't get involved.*

Turns out Olivia has news. Softened by the vodka and the intimacy which *Final Destination 2* demands, they nestle together on the sofa. Their twisted limbs – all denim and coloured socks – and sprawled bodies make for a good place to tell everything.

Nicola looks good. Her face is round and smiling and her baby weight is all gone. She has a softer look about her these days. But she doesn't like the film that much, spending most of it behind a cushion or under Ben's arm. At the end credits, when she can finally emerge, she shakes her head.

'That so sucked.'

Olivia giggles and reaches for the bottle which is between Ben's feet. 'You are such a chicken, Nic. You hardly saw any of it.'

Nicola smiles and holds her phone aloft. 'I had childcare to organize.'

Ben lifts his head. 'Jonty again? He has her a lot now doesn't he?'

Olivia pours the vodka studiously; she takes far too much time and attention over the act. Ben waits for her to speak. He knows her so well. Knows, by the furrows above her eyebrows that she's about to say something. 'It's called taking responsibility,' Ben. He has to learn. He's had her every Sunday for a few weeks now. He's getting quite good at it.'

Ben slides a look at Nicola but her eyes are wide in agreement. He remains unconvinced. 'Isn't it just called 'revenge'?'

Nicola shoves him in the ribs and overacts her gasp, 'Benjamin, what are you suggesting? Are you calling my daughter a form of punishment?'

Ben sighs and lowers his eyes. He knows how strong these two are when they're united. He even likes it. Lowering his voice to add some seriousness. 'You know I'm not.

'She's amazing.'

'Jonty's all right with her now.'

Ben thinks of Jonty; pictures the tiny little Eliza in those meat-joint arms. These days he tolerates him. Accepts that he's a part of Nicola and Olivia's lives. Even so, he can't help thinking he's a piece of shit. Hates how he treated Olivia and how he still inflicts low-lying bullying all around school. Shits like him cause so much pain but get away with murder. Olivia, as far as Ben is concerned, made the best decision of her life by blowing him out.

Nicola shrugs. Her mouth opens then closes but she doesn't say anything. The room is suddenly charged. Ben swings his legs. 'I don't know why you stayed with him for so long Livvy. He was horrible to you.'

Olivia closes her eyes. Sighs. 'Yeah, he was.' She nods slowly, Ben watches her fingers knit together. 'And sometimes he hurt me.'

Nicola's eyes widen, 'What, physically?'

Olivia nods. Ben grimaces. He'd thought as much.

'Not badly,' Olivia says quickly, 'but I never really got why.'

'How often?'

Olivia sighs, her eyes glitter. 'It started last year. He used to pinch me under my hair, at the back of my neck. And other places.' She's in full swing now. It's like she's in a trance.

Ben hates it. But has to listen.

'A couple of times he hit me around the head.' She lifts her eyes fleetingly. 'I actually saw stars when he did that. Like they say in the films.'

Nicola's mouth is O-shaped, her eyes round and frightened. 'But the hair pulling was the worst. That happened the most, usually because of something I was wearing or if I was talking to a boy.'

He hates the way her fingers are twisting round themselves. Wants to wrap his arms around her.

'I kept meaning to say something, I kept meaning to put a stop to it. It made me feel ashamed.' She exhales a wobble of breath. 'But he was always so nice afterwards. So kind of tender and sorry. I always knew he felt bad. And besides, there was never a mark or blood or even a bruise.'

'God, Livvy. I had no idea.' Nicola's face is stricken. Like she's missed the worst, most obvious secret in the world. 'What a bastard.'

'I knew it was wrong, but I didn't know how to stop it.' Nicola stares at Ben. 'Did you know?'

Shakes his head. 'I sometimes wondered. He's pretty messed up.'

Olivia agrees. 'Yeah, when his mum left he went all weird. He got angry. He took it out on other people.'

Ben grimaces. 'So he turned the tables and started bullying everyone else. It's no excuse though.'

Nicola's eyebrows rise under her fringe. She turns to Olivia. 'And you still stayed with him? I can't believe that.'

Olivia lowers her chin on to her chest. 'It sounds stupid, but sometimes he was all I had. He was all I knew. I thought this happened everywhere. His mum leaving like she did and my mum being so worried about Alice and . . . sometimes it was nice to know that I had someone whenever I wanted. Someone who loved me.' She searches Ben's eyes. 'And most of the time he was really nice to me. Made me feel special.'

Ben thinks hard. He wants to say so many things: about how slapping someone around isn't love. How sleeping with your best friend isn't making anyone feel special. But he can sense Nicola cringing beside him, pushing herself into the cushions, so he takes a breath and stops himself.

Leave it. Don't spoil it now they're back together again.

One more question then he'll have to change the subject. Things have got too heavy. 'What about Eliza? Do you still want him near her?'

Both girls look at each other; pass a glance which he doesn't really understand.

'I don't think he'll be like that with her. I think it was more a girlfriend thing. I just think he was incredibly jealous. Besides, he swears blind he doesn't do that sort of thing any more. Says he's getting help.' She puts her hand on Nicola's. Nicola nods silently. Thoughts whirring round her eyes like one-armed bandits. 'I think he's changed.'

Nobody says anything.

Olivia breaks the silence. With a sniff and an exaggerated toss of her hair she suddenly smiles, like she's just unearthed some treasure. 'Besides . . .' She narrows her eyes drawing in both Ben and Nicola '. . . he's not the only one who's changed.' She grins. 'I might have moved on.'

Immediately, Ben sits upright. 'What's that supposed to mean?'

'Oh my God!' says a delighted Nicola. 'With Blake?' The change in atmosphere is like a whirlwind.

Deliberately knocking back the last of her vodka, with the timing of a pro, Olivia looks back from one friend's expectant face to the next. Her grin widens by the second. She even closes her eyes for added affect. 'We-ell it just so happens that on the way to Biology last week, a certain Blake Johnson finally asked me out. We're official.'

Ben wonders if his eardrums may get perforated by the high-pitched screeching coming from Nicola. He's not quite sure who is the most excited. But actually, in the end, it really doesn't matter. He's pleased for her. Pleased she's found somebody else and pleased she's back with Nicola. Back to their solid little triangle. It's a good feeling.

So he pours himself another vodka.

'It's my birthday in a fortnight. Can you get a babysitter, Nic? I was thinking Nando's and a film . . . you, me and Livvy, like old times.'

Nicola flicks her hair and grimaces. 'I'll see what I can do. I'm a bit skint right now . . .' she raises her eyebrows, 'as I'm sure you can imagine.'

Turns to Olivia, who is playing with her nails. 'Livvy? What about you?'

Olivia sighs and starts to look anxious, it doesn't feel good under his skin. 'Sorry, I'm busy on the Friday and Saturday and Mum won't let me out on the Sunday because I have an exam on the Monday. You know what she's like.'

Ben pushes the fleshy part of his finger where he thinks a

194

spot will develop underneath his eye. It hurts. But who cares? Nobody will be around to notice whether he's spotty on his birthday anyhow. He tries not to feel disappointed and let-down. Things have changed. It's only natural.

Wednesday lunchtimes are crap. Most of the kids have to fend for themselves as all the teaching staff have a meeting. The corridors and dining halls are dotted with lunchtime staff but the heavier presence of teachers is absent.

The sixth-form centre isn't usually too bad. But this Wednesday the centre is being redecorated, and all the students are kicked out into the main body of the school.

He and Olivia meet up in the noisy dining hall, they have both forgotten what a hellhole the place can be, and they're both relieved when, two baguettes later, they make their way out of the room.

They deposit themselves in the computer suite where Olivia has some coursework to finish. Ben dumps his jacket on the seat next to her. 'I'll meet you back here. Just going for a piss.'

'Nice.' Olivia moans, but is now concentrating upon her password. 'See you in a minute.'

Ben saunters through the corridor, his mind on Josh. Imagining that full mouth. Picturing the back of his neck as he left the cafe on Saturday. It was a pale slash of skin which looked like it had only recently seen the light of day. As if he'd just had his hair cut. He wonders, with a lump in his throat, what it would be like to press his lips on that small patch of skin.

He doesn't see Jonty and his mates lined either side of the toilet door. His mind is too far gone.

It's only when he hears, 'Faggot alert,' that he looks up in surprise. He sees the smirk of a kid in the year below with yellow teeth and thin lips.

He rolls his eyes. He's heard it all before. But it doesn't stop the twist in his belly.

But he *is* surprised to see the broad shadow of Jonty hover in the corner of his eyeline and then, for some unexplained reason, make steps in the other direction. Ben thinks he looks like he's escaping. Running off.

'Watch your backs boys,' one of the bright sparks nearer the door shouts as Ben pushes it open. 'Gay-Boy Ben is entering the building.'

With the taste of bile at the back of his throat and a scowl which he discovers in the mirror, Ben takes his piss. Twats like these can ruin your day. And if he's not careful, that is exactly what they'll do. So, with a sniff which stings his nostrils because there's a bucket of disinfectant in the corner of the room, he aims to brazen it out.

Taking a breath and shoving open the door he grins at Yellow Teeth. 'No one in there I fancied mate. He looks Yellow Teeth up and down and adds, 'And no one out here either.'

The jeers of laughter make Yellow Teeth blush a plum colour. His sneer slides off his face and Ben watches anger light up his eyes

He walks through the wall of laughter, grinning as he goes. He hates everything about these boys, but won't for the life of him let it show.

But Yellow Teeth isn't happy. He has too much at stake. He follows Ben through the gap, anger packing his upper arms, and shoves Ben in the back.

Ben stumbles, the jab taking him by surprise. His bag slides off his shoulder and a grunt is forced from his throat. He doesn't fall to the floor but one of his knees lowers to within centimetres of it.

He's surprised.

Yellow Teeth at last has some sort of lead. He bellows so that the words echo around the corridor. 'Fucking queer.'

And with a boot worthy of any Premiership football player, he kicks at Ben's bag so that it slides from one end of the corridor to the other.

It slides to a halt against some feet in Nikes belonging to Josh Strong. He's standing against the door to the Art room, a half-eaten sandwich in his hand. Josh looks from the bag on the floor up to Ben's face.

Ben flushes wildly, his heart lurches and his breath stings the back of his throat.

This wasn't how our next meeting was meant to be.

Two days later, at the end of school, he sees Josh walking out of Science. There are three girls between them. Josh is alone, his head down, looking at his phone. Ben glimpses the white of the back of his neck. Feels the familiar pull at the bottom of his stomach. He thinks about skirting round the girls, matching Josh stride for stride. Maybe making him laugh.

He starts to visualize it. Holds his breath. His heart begins to hammer at the thought.

Speeds up his steps.

But then, as a bus pulls in and the girls lift their eyes, they say some words which turn Josh's head. He grins at them. One of them grabs at Josh's blazer.

Josh dips his head towards her and she follows him up the steps of the bus. Ben watches from the pavement, his steps now slow again. He sees through the darkened window, as they find a seat near the front. How the girl slides an earphone into Josh's ear. How their heads bow together as they share some music. How their knees are up against the seats in front. Their ankles jiggling together to the music.

Ben knows he's not been noticed, standing there on the pavement.

Ridiculous. Why would he even like me anyhow?

Nicola texts when he's just finishing work at seven. It's a weird text, one which scratches at his throat. Unusual; has him slightly baffled.

Ben

You OK Babe? x he replies.

Yeah. Don't spose you're free tonight? x

He unties his apron. Knows it needs a wash. He'll think about taking it home next week. Janey's a bit of a stickler for clean aprons. He hangs it on the peg. Thumbs his response.

As it happens, that party I was going to . . . it's been cancelled x

Quickly, like she's been holding on to the phone, there's a reply.

Fancy coming round? Mum's out. x

Shrugs on his jacket. It's denim and cost a small fortune, even though it's vintage. Worry nags behind his eyebrows.

Sure. You OK? x

Three seconds where he imagines her fingers flashing over her phone.

I'm fine. All good. Only I wanted a word. x

Narrows his eyes, pushes open the door. He yells over his shoulder. 'See you next week, Janey.'

He hears the muffled reply from where she's mopping the floor. 'Don't do anything I wouldn't.' Shakes his head. She's a laugh is Janey.

He steps out into the evening, feels the weight of his phone in his hand. He senses importance in its heaviness.

Be there in twenty. Pour us a drink. I'm gagging. x

Feels funny. Nicola rarely does this. Springing suggestions like this. Since Eliza's been born everything's been planned weeks in advance. She's moaned about how spontaneity is a thing of the past. It's unnerving. Gets his mind thinking spirals.

The walk's a fast one, through the copse under trees which whisper at him. Over the bridge, his creepers thumping on the planks. Into the park with straggling kids shouting for the ball. Past Josh's house. All quiet and dark. No sign of Josh to speed up his heart. Past the supermarket with a gang of lads jeering and laughing. Thinks he sees Jonty. Ducks his head. Doesn't want a conversation. Not tonight. Paces into Nicola's cul-de-sac. Decides to slow his steps. There's no need for a breathless entrance.

Calm down.

Stops for a fag. Needs one. Under the lamp post, sucking up the nicotine. Can't get the weirdness from under his skin.

She probably just wants some company. It must be lonely on a Saturday night with a baby on your own. With the thought of everyone else getting ready to go out.

Stubs at his cigarette with the toe of his shoe. Breathes in under the jabber of birds and heads for her house.

She's at the door before he can put his finger on the bell. She must have been looking out for him. The house smells of oven chips and sausages. A welcome which reminds him how hungry he is. She holds the door wide. She manages a smile, which doesn't quite meet her eyes.

'You OK?'

She nods, but he notices the twist in her hands. She points into the lounge where Eliza's on a blanket on the floor. 'You go in. I'll get that drink.'

He perches on the end of the sofa. Unpeels his jacket. Puts it to one side. Eliza's gurgling with soft pink cheeks. He smiles at her, reaches out for her fingers. They curl over his like a tiny silk sea creature. It calms him down. He grins at her. 'Lady, I reckon it's way past your bedtime.'

She smiles at him and he thinks she looks cute in her small, warm pyjamas, a fragrance of bath time and shampoo comes off her.

He looks around him at the tiny lounge. Not enough room to swing a cat, let alone three females. No wonder Nicola gets frustrated sometimes.

Spots a scented candle lit on the mantelpiece. His heart ramps up a beat. *What's going on?*

Nicola comes back, a bottle of milk in one hand, what looks like cider in the other. He sees the fizz of bubbles surge to the surface. Nicola's mouth looks tight. There's a smile thrown over the back of the sofa to him, but it still doesn't touch her eyes.

There's a throb at the back of his throat.

She nods to Eliza on the floor. 'I was keeping her up. I thought you might want to see her.'

'Always – she's completely perfect.' He sees a flash of something in her eyes.

'Not at three o'clock in the morning she's not.'

He squeezes his forehead. 'It's not fair that it's always you.'

She shrugs. 'My choice.'

'Shouldn't the dad have to do something?'

A small line forms between her eyes as she bends to lift Eliza on to her knee. 'C'mon, you. Time for your bedtime bottle.'

He watches the soothing ritual; the baby sagging into Nicola's elbow, her eyes attached to her mum's. The button mouth ready to pull on the bottle, a tiny, soft hand lifted to graze against the plastic; a whisper of encouragement from Nicola.

Ben sips his cider and waits. Won't break the silence. He breathes in the scented candle and fidgets his feet. It's never normally awkward.

Just the soft ticking of Eliza's mouth.

But then he suddenly has to say something, feels a bubble of it form in his stomach. Coughs. 'Nic, what's this all about?' He nods at the candle. 'You're not trying to seduce me are you? Cos you know I'm a lost cause.'

She giggles – which is a godsend – and pulls out the teat from Eliza's mouth with a small pop.

'No,' but the tiny frown lines reappear when she tilts her head, 'though you weren't always.'

He swallows. This is really unusual. This is never normally talked about. That mad hour all those months ago has been buried. Buried under clods of embarrassment, hidden behind a good friendship, away from the eyes of Olivia.

'Woah! What you bringing that up for? I kind of thought we'd agreed never to talk about it again.' Hears his voice suddenly all thin and reedy. 'My disastrous, last-ditch attempt at straightness.'

Nicola lifts Eliza on to her shoulder, starts patting away at her back. It's OK though, there's at last a smile with a mischief flavour on her lips. 'Cheeky shit. That last-ditch attempt was my virginity.'

He laughs. Ducks his head. Feels shivers. Remembers the fumbles. Remembers their drunkenness; the mess of clothes and the taste of disappointment. In her bedroom while her mum was downstairs watching *Downton Abbey*. They'd been drinking all day. Stolen vodka from Olivia's dad's drinks cabinet. Dutch courage, and an agreement – to get shot of their virginities. A mess. A disastrous, horrible mess which set his mind straight once and for all. He was gay. One hundred per cent.

'Oops.'

Eliza's drowsy. Her legs have slumped, frog-shaped against Nicola. She looks the picture of sated baby. 'I need to take her up.' She stands, places the empty bottle on the table next to his cider. Nods to the stairs. 'Want to come?'

'Um, OK.'

The bedroom's dark. Already prepared for a sleeping baby. Curtains drawn, floor cleared for walking on. Nicola's bed all made up ready for slipping into. The cot's empty, save a small, purple cloth rabbit in the corner.

He looks at it all this. She's brilliant is Nicola. A really good mum. This happy, sleeping baby is proof. Ben swells with pride. Leans against the door frame watching them. There's a small sigh from the sleeping baby. It's lovely. Really lovely.

Nicola straightens after fussing a bit over the side of the cot. She pushes her shoulders back, stands upright.

'I've never been good at maths, Ben.'

'What?'

'I've never been good at dates and things.'

'That's OK. You don't need to, to get into the fashion business . . . do you?' She's starting to confuse him. Doesn't like the shake in her hands.

'She's got blue eyes.'

He frowns. 'I know, like Jonty.'

'So have you.'

His whole body is pinned against the door frame now. Something's fixing him there. There's a pulse in the side of his throat. 'Um . . . what are you trying to say, Nicola?'

Her hand is on the side of the cot but the rest of her has turned to face him. He's never seen her look so serious. Her hair falls, all waves on her shoulders. 'I'm saying that I think I may have got it wrong, Ben. That when I worked it out with the calendar last week, like I should have done before, the dates don't match.' She looks back at the cot. 'They don't match for Jonty.' And then she whispers so that he can't really hear her. But it doesn't matter. He knows, like a siren – an alarm-triggering, skin-prickling distress signal – what she's saying. 'But they do match for you.'

The words sock him in the stomach. Sock at him like a mallet.

'You think she might be . . . be mine?'

She nods. Bites her bottom lip.

'Oh God. But what about Jonty?'

She moves to the bed. Perches on the end like her legs can't hold her any more. Her teeth are gnawing at her lip. It starts to look sore. She speaks between her fingers.

'I was stupid. I just went along with it like everybody else. I think because you and me . . . well, it was only the once and neither of us really remembers it. And it was such a disaster. I think, because me and Jonty did it four times . . .'

'Shit, Nic. I can't . . .' Swallows great globs of shock. 'I can't

204

believe what you're saying.'

There's a roar inside his head then. Like being in a cave and having a crash of the sea echo and collapse. The wave splatters and collides against the side of his scalp, so it hurts.

His foot is tapping on the threadbare carpet. Can't seem to swallow. Can't seem to breathe. There's another crash of the wave and he wishes he was sitting down like Nicola.

He slumps on to the floor.

Knows she's staring. He can feel her eyes lasering him.

The baby . . . *his* baby stirs in her sleep. The mallet socks at him again.

Thinks fleetingly of the cider downstairs. Of tripping down the steps; of the coolness of the liquid; of the alcohol burning down his throat. He could down it; swing open the front door and run outside into the still-light evening air. Nobody would know any different. Parties could still be had. It would only take a few quick texts and he'd find a way of spending his Saturday night. Nobody would know any different.

Except Nicola. Nicola with the heart-shaped mouth; with the concerned look and the words which have just battered at his insides.

He knows he's got to say something. The room is bursting with the expectation of it.

'Um . . .'

He's never lost for words. His English teacher says he's too full of them.

She squeezes her nose with pinched fingers. She won't take his eyes off him. 'Ben?'

'How can you be sure?' Hates himself.

With a disappointed drop of the head, so he feels even worse. 'It was nine months and two days before she was born.' She looks at him then. He doesn't like the hardness in her eyes. 'The first time I slept with Jonty was seven months and three days.' She smoothes her hands over her thighs. 'And she wasn't premature. She was a healthy, full-term baby.'

'How did you—?'

She looks up again. Her eyes glitter with tears. 'My health visitor. She's good. She does more than she should. I think because I'm seventeen she's allowed to do more visits.' She shrugs. 'I don't know.' She pushes her lips with her finger. He wants to tell her to stop doing that. 'So last week, we were talking about conception and stuff. So that it doesn't happen again. Not till I want it to. About the menstrual cycle and ovulation.' She winces. 'Sorry, is this too much information?'

He manages to shake his head.

'So we got out the calendar from last year and she made me go through it. Showed me about dates. I mean we learnt about it in Biology, didn't we? I should have known. But all that was a bit sciency, not really about me. So she said that the best way to learn was to look at it yourself. Know your own body and stuff. Kind of apply it to you. Does that make sense?'

Nodding. It's all he can do right now.

'And it's when we did that that I suddenly realized that the dates don't add up. Not with Jonty.'

There's a silence in the room which is noisy as it clashes against the walls.

206

He stands up. Takes another look at Eliza. She's on her back, her hands either side of her head. Surrendering. Peaceful.

It's difficult to swallow. Difficult to breathe.

'Jonty'll go crazy.'

She nods. 'But what about you?'

'Um . . . Nic, this is a bit hard to take in. Um . . . Can I have a minute? You know, to get my head together.'

She drops her head quickly so that her hair falls like a curtain round her face. He feels bad. Really bad. 'Look, I believe you. Don't get me wrong . . . only . . . um . . .'

Hates himself. Hate, hate, hate.

She stands up. All sharp. 'OK. Look, why don't you go? Go and have a think. It's OK. I've had a week to think about this. I'm sorry. Sorry for springing this on you . . .'

'I'll be all right. I'll help and stuff, only I'm a bit . . . you know . . .'

They're bustling to the door. Jostling for the stairs. Awkward elbows and knees. He can't get out quick enough. Desperate for air. Gagging to get outside.

Clashes against the front door, fumbles for the latch. Hears the solid crunch of it as it closes behind him.

At the end of the path, when he's sure she's not looking, he leans over. Rests his hands on his thighs. Breathes ragged, painful gasps. Hair in his eyes.

Don't be sick, not here.

'Did you have a nice time?' Bella's hand is in his. It's small and soft, her fingers grip tightly as they cross the road.

She skips up the curb. 'We had burgers. Tia's mum is a great cook. She does curly chips.'

Ben smiles. Bella judges everyone by what they offer to eat.

'Curly chips, eh?'

She giggles. 'And pink sauce.'

They're walking home on his birthday evening. He tries not to feel sorry for himself. It's not Olivia's fault she was busy on his birthday. The card and Rolling Stones T-shirt more than make up for it. But even so, she's been his friend for a while now and he can't help feeling hurt. He wonders what she's doing. What's more important than seeing a mate on their birthday?

It's eight o'clock. The time when he should be getting ready for going out, like everyone else on their birthdays. Instead he's been made to collect his sister from her own celebrations with her five-year-old friend.

His head is full of Nicola and Eliza. He's had a week to think of her news. Can't get them from under his skin. He's phoned her a couple of times. Told her he's OK. Reassured her that he understands. That he believes her. That he accepts he *is* Eliza's dad. But he's not really sure. Not really sure that he's up to this. That stupid, drunken fling proved what exactly? Something he knew already. And then Eliza. He's still reeling with it, despite what he's said. But he loves them. Loves them both. And he'd never let them down. Nicola's brilliant these days – so strong. But she still needs all the support she can get. And if it means it has to come from him, then so be it. But fatherly support? Well, that's something completely different.

And he still can't get his head round it.

Goes to sleep worrying about it. Wakes up early with it still there. A pounding pebble of fret.

'And ice cream with strawberry sauce.' His sister is still reeling off the menu. Any other time and it'd make him laugh.

The house is surprisingly gloomy when they walk up the path. The windows are blank and unwelcoming; it looks somehow bare. He frowns. Feels Bella's reticence in her fingers. She loiters reluctantly behind his legs. 'Where is everyone?'

He feels for his keys. 'Maybe they've gone out?' His voice sounds unnaturally loud in the silence. He's aware of his sister's sudden fear. 'I'll give Mum a ring when we get in.'

Inside he can't understand why there are no lights on. His mum always leaves the lamp on in the hallway. He stretches his fingers to where the lamp should be. Everything feels strange.

Alarm trickles up his back. Something's not right.

Bella trembles in the doorway. 'Ben?' Her voice quavers.

'Stay there,' he demands and reaches for a stick by the front door which his stepdad uses when he goes walking.

And then, all of a sudden, there's a flash of light and a yell which has stars prickling at the back of his head.

'Surprise!'

It's a multi-voiced shriek which makes him jump several centimetres off the laminate. Bella leaps to the back of his knees, her little arms circling around his thighs.

And so it's in this ridiculous pose, with him brandishing a

stick and his sister round his legs that he greets a room full of grinning, laughing friends.

Out of the haze of faces and teeth and party poppers shooting off in all directions, he first spots his mum, then Olivia, then Nicola.

Relief and shock fizz through him. He drops the stick and finally realizes what's happening: he's been had. He'd been sent out to collect his sister so that a shedload of mates could come round and surprise him. He didn't know he had so many friends. And suddenly a grin as wide as the moon splits his face.

A birthday surprise.

'You bastards.' He laughs, then clamps his fingers over his mouth as he remembers his sister is there.

Then there are hugs. Great, perfumed, smiling, lovely hugs which thrill his insides. The noise is deafening and Bella has folded on to the floor in shock. Someone cranks up some music in the living room and his mum stands proudly by his side, scooping up Bella, telling her that everything's all right.

'Mum?' he sighs. 'You did this?'

She shakes her head. 'Not me.' She nods over to Olivia and Nicola. 'This is all their doing. I'm just providing the venue.' Olivia grins and moves close to him so that he can breathe in her honey fragrance. 'You honestly thought we'd forget your birthday?' she shouts over the music.

'The T-shirt . . . ?'

She smiles, winding her arms round his neck. 'Just a clever ploy.'

He shakes his head. 'I hate you.'

She smiles so she feels the bulge of her cheek against his. 'I don't care, because I love you.'

He pulls her to him. 'I can't believe this.' He looks over her shoulder at the crowd of friends who are now moving to the living room. The music is too strong a pull.

He counts at least thirty friends. Mostly from school, a couple from the cafe. Their shadowy figures make a party scene, where only an hour earlier there was just his mum and stepdad.

Someone shoves a can of lager in his hand and he thinks of the shirt hanging in his wardrobe which he would like to wear rather than the scruffy hoodie that he's got on at the moment.

People throw their arms around him. He can't stop grinning. It's like frogs are bounding behind his eyes.

Nicola grabs his arm and pulls him down on to the sofa. She clutches his arm and smiles warmly. 'You OK, honey?'

He nods at her. The awkwardness from last week fades off her face. 'We'll chat later, yeah?'

Relief seeps through him. She's tapping away at his arm, determined to be bright. 'Your mum's been brilliant.' She yells in his ear. 'She's agreed to leave us to it. She won't be back until midnight.' She nods at a stack of cans. 'She's even bought some drinks.'

He swallows. He's always known his mum was the best person in the world. Tries not to think about how she's going to react when he tells her his news. 'What about Bella and Dave?'

Nicola nods. She's looking cute in a short dress which pulls tight over her curves. He can't get over how much she's changed since Eliza's been born. Instead of just being Olivia's friend, it's almost like she's the strongest person he now knows.

She carries on. 'They're going too. Think they're going to your grandma's.'

He sinks his head against the back of the sofa and sighs. *This is happiness.* This is worth every bit of the misery he's experienced in the last fortnight.

Olivia stands in front of him. Her cheeks are pink and shiny and she looks lush in a shorts-and-tights combo. She puts her head to one side knowingly. 'You want to go and change, don't you?'

He groans – only Olivia would realize this. 'You know me too well.'

She points a ballet pump at his shin. 'Yeah. I know what a vain little shit you are.'

Later, feeling properly dressed and smelling like he should at a party, he goes downstairs. Music still thuds from the living room. Kids from school sway from one room to the next. It's hard to take in. Wonders about Josh. Hopes he's been invited.

He spots Seb from the cafe talking to Dan from History. The football crew are dancing with Nicola and Mel from his old Science class in front of a pile of DVDs for five-year-olds.

Ben's world, it seems, has gone very, very mad.

But it's a good mad.

He takes another drink from the table and looks around. Music. Good music. Music from his iPod. And people are actually dancing to it.

The French windows bang open as somebody slides through. He smells the scent of cigarettes. He'd like one.

He spots Josh Strong wading through the throng of figures between the kitchen and living room. Ben's mouth turns dry as he catches his eye. He slaps Ben on the back 'Happy Birthday, mate,' he shouts, his breath warm on Ben's face. There's a stab of something hot at the back of his throat. Josh scrubs Ben's head and moves along, some girl from English clinging on to his arm and laughing. Ben can't say anything. Just ducks his head.

He walks past the kitchen table which is littered with cards. Cards which must be for him.

After a cigarette and a can of beer, he slides into the corner of the kitchen where Olivia is standing. She smiles. 'You enjoying yourself?'

He nods. 'Thanks, Livvy. This is the best.'

She's had just enough to drink, he realizes, to be even softer than normal. She swigs from a glass and speaks in his ear. 'I hated it when we weren't friends.'

'Me too.'

'Promise it won't happen again?'

He slips his hand around her waist. 'Promise.'

'I love you, Ben,' she says again. And he knows whatever

happens, this love will be there for life.

They stand softly against the kitchen cabinets, watching the party unwind around them. His hand stays attached to her warm skin. Jonty walks into the room, followed by Nicola. They're laughing. He's holding a bottle of cider high above her head; she's reaching for it so Jonty lifts it higher. There's something in the air around them. It crackles. Ben feels Olivia breathe in beside him. He nudges her gently. 'You OK?'

She nods quickly, perhaps too quickly. Then smiles. 'She's changing, isn't she?'

'Yeah.'

She leans into him. 'But it's a good change, isn't it? I mean, she was always clothes, clothes, clothes. But now, since Eliza,' shakes her head. 'I dunno . . . it's like she's more happy underneath the clothes.'

He knows this is hard to say. Loves her for it. Watches as Jonty finally hands the drink over to Nicola and she takes a swig. His eyes are softer than Ben's ever seen.

Winces. Thinks about the new ball of knowledge sitting in his stomach. He's sure Jonty will flip. Can't imagine the conversation. Won't think about it. It's his party. His birthday. Olivia and Nicola have gone to all the trouble.

Sighs, turns away from the way Jonty and Nicola are now openly flirting in the middle of the room. Pulls Olivia through to the living room. 'C'mon. Let's dance.'

The jabber of voices over music. The flicker of candle light. The smell of wine and beer and cider. The feel of warm fingers and hands and hair everywhere he goes. The Stone Roses.

Echo & the Bunnymen. Killing Joke. The Clash. INXS. All his favourite bands.

Dancing. Maybe to forget: punching his fist into the air to 'Teenage Dirtbag'. All thirty-two of them in one room. Like the crest of a wave. Thirty-two beautifully formed fists under the lights, like thirty-two pink creatures. Dancing with Olivia who kicks off her shoes because they hurt. One lands in the warm space between the back of the sofa and Sam Rhodes's neck where he's passed out, his mouth open with a slick of saliva glistening down his cheek. Dancing with the football crew to Public Enemy; shoulders shoving, feeling the warmth of Josh Strong's palms on his back. Looking at him, diamonds of sweat dangling from the dark strands of his hair. Laughing as he shakes like a dog so that Ben can taste the salt. Dancing, dancing, dancing.

He finds himself pulled down on to the sofa. Warm fingers in his hand. Nicola. All fragrant of musky body spray and shampoo, her cheeks high with colour, her eyelashes dark against shining eyes. She's smiling next to the passed-out Sam Rhodes. Her dress clings to a gently rising stomach, not even a reminder of the baby. She has to shout in his ear for the noise.

'Sorry again about last week – springing it on you like that.'

He shrugs, shifts against her. Smells her warmth. His lips against her ear, 'S'OK. You had to tell me somehow.'

'How'd you feel about it today?'

'Still a bit shit.' He fiddles with her fingers. 'Why didn't we use a condom, Nic?'

She sighs, crosses her legs, flexes and points her toes. 'You were off your face.' Grimaces. 'So was I. We're the original teenage cliché.'

Some Nirvana through the speakers. The room gets clogged again. A wave of bouncing friends. Some sweat. Waves of cider. Flashes of skin where tops come out of jeans. From down on the sofa he can swim in the glow of the party. He'd like to dance. Knows he can't. Not with the conversation still going.

'What shall I do?'

She presses his fingers. 'You don't have to do very much for now. Just carry on being you. Stick with me. Help me now and again. We'll work something out.'

Hears a shake in his voice. 'I can't believe I actually have a daughter.'

She smiles. It fills her face. She's got no idea how pretty she is. 'You have.'

In the corner, slightly away from the dancing, by the television in a small animal huddle are Jonty and two of his friends. They're big, they're laughing and they're drinking. There's the knot of knowledge again, at the base of his stomach. Ben jabs his toe towards the corner. 'There's our biggest problem.' Jonty's grinning wide at something his mate has just said. He senses Nicola's sigh next to him.

'I know. I'm not sure what to do there.'

'He'll freak.'

'I know.'

'He's just got used to the idea. Just started to come round.'

'I know. And he's actually quite good at it.'

Pulls a face. 'You sure?'

'Yeah . . . surprisingly.'

'It'll mess with his head. He'll go ape-shit.'

He feels a quiver in her fingers. 'I know.'

'So what the hell are we going to do, Nic?'

Glances at her profile. Sees the eyelashes close. 'Do you mind . . . do you mind if we keep it a secret for a bit? Till I've got my head round it. Till I've found a way of telling him.'

'Course.' There's a funny sensation of protection and fear and anxiety on his tongue. It's hard to understand. It's all so new. He sighs. 'Let me know when you've thought of a way though. Cos I reckon I'm going to need a bulletproof vest. That or a one-way ticket to Australia.'

She shakes her head. 'He's not that bad.'

She's wrong. He's certain of that. But right now it's not worth telling her. Instead, he lets Nirvana thrash through his living room and vibrate through the sofa.

Much later, there are empty bottles everywhere. Every surface seems to be covered in party debris. Ben wanders outside. He thinks about a cigarette but likes the idea of just sitting there in the darkness with the jostle of voices through the living-room window. There's so much to think about.

He grins to himself. Peers up into the bright dots of stars pin-pricking the night sky. Doesn't hear the back door open. Closes his eyes in contentment.

The creak of the bench where he's sitting has him opening

his eyes and fumbling for his cigarettes. Josh's pine fragrance hits Ben before he even realizes who it is.

'All right?' Josh grins and settles himself on the bench.

Ben pulls a half smile and lights up. Josh's knee bumps against Ben's thigh. It burns. 'Yeah.'

He smokes quietly, watching the stars, feeling the whole of his left side tingle.

Josh inhales. Seems to start to say something then stops. Ben swallows.

Finally: 'You sometimes stare at me, you know?' Said quietly. Half a mumble.

Ben feels a blush flash on to his cheeks. He takes a hurried drag and squeezes his eyes in embarrassment. 'Um, yeah, sorry.' Josh shakes his head quickly. 'No – it's OK.'

A cheer of something in the house through the windows. Laughter rippling through the party. It's going on without them. That's OK. Ben likes the idea of all these people in his house while he's sitting out here with Josh.

Prickles of tension.

And then, before either of them say anything else and before Ben can even sense it, Josh reaches over and kisses him. On the lips. Firmly planted on his mouth. Ben lifts his chin and kisses him back.

The kiss says the thousand things that he can't find the words to say.

It isn't very long. Josh draws back and Ben takes a final pull on his cigarette then flicks it on to the floor where it smoulders gently.

There's a fog of embarrassment. In the corner of Ben's eye he sees Josh flex his fingers. His knee is still blazing into Ben's thigh.

The dart of a silent owl wings its way across the width of the garden. Josh shakes his shoulders. He stuffs his hands under his thighs. 'I've never done that before . . . with a boy, I mean.'

Ben holds his breath, winces. 'Me neither.'

Josh raises his eyebrows but doesn't push the point. He turns to Ben. 'You want to come to mine sometime? Next week maybe? We can watch a film or go on the Xbox?'

Ben coughs in surprise.

'You don't have to, if you don't want to?'

Ben smiles. Then nods his head. He can feel his cheeks swell until it feels like they might burst. He nods again. 'Yeah – OK.'

Josh gets up. He brushes his thighs with the palms of his hand. Ben likes Josh's hands. They're solid but signal so much information. He jerks his head back into the house. 'Well, I'd best get back in.'

Ben nods. Inhales. Nods again. 'Yeah, I'll be there in a bit.'

He watches Josh's back as he saunters out of the light into the gasp of the party.

He leans his head back against the wall and the graze of the brickwork snags at his hair. He's happy. In love.

In love with this boy; in love with his friends . . . and now . . . in love with his baby.

His blood and his breath are buzzing with it.

ACKNOWLEDGEMENTS

I haven't done this on my own. From the moment I started thinking about this book I've been in partnership with someone. I'm going to start with Dan Tunstall. He was before *The Baby* – he was my inspiration. His book, *Big & Clever*, got me so inspired that I wanted to write a book there and then – literally walk out of the library where I was working and start within seconds of being at my computer. He gave me years of support and encouragement. I'll never forget that.

Thanks to Leicester Writing School. They brought me together with some fantastic authors and writers. Writing's a bit solitary. That's why it's good to sit with others who are doing the same thing. I enjoyed those courses.

Then the sublime Writing East Midlands. Winning a place on their Mentoring Scheme was wonderful, but then pairing me up with the Great and Godly Maxine Linnell was their true stroke of genius. Maxine is brilliant. We worked so hard on getting this book right. Loads of coffee, loads of rewrites and most importantly loads of laughs. Wow, Maxine, you are the wisest woman I know. Truly, truly, thank you. (You getting bored of me saying it yet?)

Then, of course, to Chicken House. To Barry Cunningham, Rachel Hickman and Rachel Leyshon who made me feel welcome from the start and who gave me stacks of advice while always ensuring *The Baby* remained mine. Their emails and phone calls continue to make me smile, but Rachel Leyshon's 'twist' phone call was the best. She was so nervous at the suggestion. And I didn't stop laughing for hours afterwards. It was a genius idea, Rachel. Thank you.

I got my inspiration for *The Baby* from *The Slap*. I loved the structure and hoped I could do something similar for young adults. So thank you for writing it, Christos Tsiolkas.

Thanks to Mum, Dad, Jan and Bill. They have always been there with their interest and support. Mum started my enjoyment of books right from when I was little – taking me to a library that I eventually ended up working in. And Dad, well, he taught me how to be determined and strong. Thank you.

To Kate, Owen and Rob. Rob for his relentless support, peeling me off the ceiling for the good news, pulling me from the depths of despair for the bad. Kate for being my first reader. She's plucky for a daughter – never worrying that her criticism might result in a major-league mum-sulk. And Owen for our fights over the computer, where he almost always let me win. Thank you, lovely little family. X

To my brothers Alister and Peter and my wonderful sisters-in-law Julie and Su. To Jill, Paul, Keith and Karen – thank you for your interest and enthusiasm. Alister recommended *The Slap* to me in amongst a shedload of other 'interesting' books. Julie, you have my back – I know it, and it's a lovely feeling.

To three people who won't ever read this – Dan, Karen and Eurydd. You might not be here any more – but I still talk to you and I know you'd be happy for me.

Thank you to all my friends, old and new. I'm blown away by your support, enthusiasm, interest and suggestions. You're all blimmin' wonderful. To Sarah L and Sherralyn for not laughing when I told you, all those years back, that this was what I wanted to do. Your love, friendship, coffees and wine have kept me going.

To the staff and friends at Leicestershire Libraries for letting me work in such a fabulously inspiring environment. (It's also where I first borrowed *The Slap*.)

To my teaching colleagues past and present – I always threatened to do this. And to my students who continually make me smile – thank you.

And finally to my sparkly new agent, Anna Power, who I hope is going to help me keep up with this writing lark.

Thank you, brilliant people. I hope you enjoy my baby, called *The Baby*, which has been my actual baby for over a year now. It has given me sleepless nights and has spent the best part of its life under a blanket. But now it's time to rock up to playgroup, throw open the doors and let someone else see the tantrums. Let me know what you think.

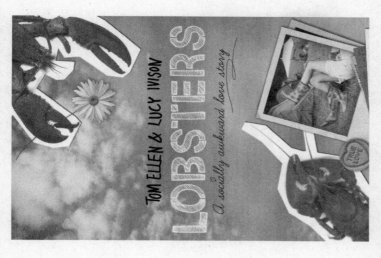

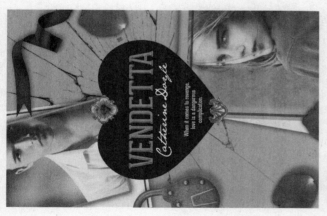

VENDETTA by CATHERINE DOYLE

For Sophie, it's a long, dull summer in the Chicago suburbs, until five mysterious brothers move into her neighbourhood. A chance encounter with one of them leaves her breathless. But as the secrets of Nic's Sicilian heritage emerge, Sophie's new world shatters. Now she realizes that the choice between love and family comes at a deadly price.

'The sexy bad boy and his distorted sense of honour will . . . have adolescent girls rooting for the wrong 'uns in this Romeo and Juliet of the underworld.'

DAILY MAIL

'. . . a novel that will keep its readers turning the pages.'

THE IRISH TIMES

Paperback, ISBN: 978-1-909489-81-3, £7.99 • ebook, ISBN 978-1-909489-82-0, £7.99